Christmas at
WAPOS BAY

Christmas at WAPOS BAY

JORDAN WHEELER
& DENNIS JACKSON

COTEAU
BOOKS
FOR KIDS

FROM MANY
PEOPLES

Edited by Barbara Sapergia.
Cover images: *background:* ©FirstLight, *models:* photographed by Paul Austring, *l to r:* Frederick Daigneault, Justyn James Levi Challis, and Ember Jade LaRose .
Cover montage and book design by Duncan Campbell.
Printed and bound in Canada by Gauvin Press

Library and Archives Canada Cataloguing in Publication

Wheeler, Jordan, 1964-
Christmas at Wapos Bay / Jordan Wheeler & Dennis Jackson.

(From many peoples)
ISBN 1-55050-324-3

1. Cree Indians—Saskatchewan—Juvenile fiction. 2. Christmas stories, Canadian (English). I. Jackson, Dennis, 1968- II. Title. III. Series.

PS8595.H385C47 2005   JC813'.54   C2005-905873-0

10   9   8   7   6   5   4   3   2   1

2517 Victoria Ave.
Regina, Saskatchewan
Canada   S4P OT2

Available in Canada & the US from
Fitzhenry & Whiteside
195 Allstate Parkway
Markham, ON,   L3R 4T8

The publisher gratefully acknowledges the financial support of its publishing program by: the Saskatchewan Arts Board, the Canada Council for the Arts, the Government of Canada through the Book Publishing Industry Development Program (BPIDP), the City of Regina Arts Commission, the Saskatchewan Cultural Industries Development Fund, Saskatchewan Culture Youth and Recreation, SaskCulture Inc., Saskatchewan Centennial 2005, Saskatchewan Lotteries, and the LaVonne Black Memorial Fund.

*I would like to dedicate this book to my lovely wife,
Melanie, and our two beautiful boys, Aaron and Eric,
who were the inspiration for this story.*
— DENNIS JACKSON

*And to Bernelda Wheeler, for generously passing on, and
nurturing, the storytelling tradition.*
— JORDAN WHEELER

*This book, and the rest of the
From Many Peoples series
is dedicated to the memory of LaVonne Black.
(See page 141)*

CHAPTER ONE
First Light

The morning sun breaks over the horizon of a northern Saskatchewan lake, as the birds sing and the snow-covered land slowly turns from deep blue to brilliant yellow. The tiny suspended crystals of the ice fog glitter in the sun before the calm gives way to a breeze and the crystals are swept away on waves of moving air. A few rays filter through a stand of trees and hit a dog team nestled in the snow outside a log cabin near the shore. A sled for the dog team leans against the front wall.

Smoke rises from the cabin's chimney as the lead dog, Freedom, stirs, the sun hitting his eyelids. They flicker open and he yawns in a high-pitched whine, then shakes his head and looks at the other sleeping dogs huddled with him for warmth. All of them, including

Shadow, remain fast asleep. Freedom shifts his weight and stands up to stretch, his muscular frame pulling at the frozen harness keeping him and the other dogs tied together. He casts a long shadow across the snow. The other dogs whine as they slowly come to life and Freedom friskily paws at them as they stick their noses towards the sun and blink against the brightness.

Freedom looks over at Shadow, who stands tall and stares back at him. Freedom barks and shakes the snow off his body and the other dogs do the same, some of the snow hitting Shadow after it flies from their bodies. Shadow averts his nose and eyes and steps back, away from the group, then shakes snow off his own body. Freedom finishes and watches Shadow before he barks again, inciting the other dogs to bark as well. Shadow becomes still and stares at Freedom, who barks at him some more. The other dogs keep barking too, but at nothing in particular, as they start to play-fight. Above them a large raven lands in a tree, knocking snow off the thick branch it wraps its talons around. The raven shakes out its feathers and lets out a loud caw. The dogs look up, all startled save Freedom.

Inside the cabin, Mushom, a man in his late sixties, is already dressed and awake, his long, black and grey hair braided and hanging at the sides of his head. He sips from a steaming cup of freshly brewed coffee, staring out the window, watching the dogs come to life. Behind him in the one-room cabin sits a wood stove, double bed, two bunk beds (with three sleeping children beneath the covers), a table and eating area with pieces of bannock laid out on a plate, a kitchen area, and a storage area for wood. Among the various items for a life on the land is a crate full of furs. Handmade Christmas decorations adorn the log walls as the glow of the fire in the stove slowly gives way to the sun. Mushom lets out a soft sigh and turns.

"*Wanska,* my grandchildren. It's a good day to trap. The dogs are waiting for you." He steps over to the bunk beds where the three children remain asleep. He nudges each of them gently. "T-Bear, Talon, Raven. *Wanska!*"

The children, two boys and a younger girl, slowly stir and open their eyes, then shield them from the morning light. T-Bear rolls over and looks out the window. His cousins Talon and Raven (the girl) do the same. The wood stove crackles as Mushom moves to the frosted cabin window to look at the sunrise.

T-Bear yawns. "What time is it, Mushom?"

Mushom smiles and walks to the stove. "There are no clocks up here, T-Bear, but your father and the others should be here before the sun goes down." He pours more coffee into his mug and sets it down on the table. He grabs a large sweater off the back of the chair and puts it on as the children climb out of their beds in their pajamas. Raven and Talon approach Mushom and both give him a hug.

"Morning, Mushom," Talon says.

"Morning, Mushom," Raven repeats.

Mushom smiles at them. "Your mother and father will be here too, along with your kohkum. It is a long way from the city, you know." Talon and Raven nod and Mushom rubs their messy hair with his large hand. T-Bear, meanwhile, stares out the window.

"When are we gonna see some animals?" he asks his grandfather. "We haven't trapped anything yet."

Mushom sits on a chair and looks up thoughtfully before he takes a deep breath. "I don't know, my boy. Last summer's forest fire did a lot of damage...a lot of damage."

A sad silence fills the cabin. Raven steps over to her grandfather and looks into his kind face. "Mushom, are we going to have enough food for Christmas?" she asks.

Mushom smiles and pats Raven on the head. "We still have today and Christmas Eve," he tells her. "A good hunter is never stuck, right, Talon?"

Talon turns and smiles. "Right, Mushom!"

T-Bear walks over to the stack of furs in the wooden crate. He picks one up and strokes the soft pelt. "My dad said if you go to the Trading Post with these, we should have enough money to buy a turkey and everything."

Mushom walks over to T-Bear and takes the fur. He shakes it out and holds it up to Raven. They all see that it's not just a fur, but a coat in Raven's size. "My grandchildren need warm clothes for Christmas more than the Trading Post needs these furs," Mushom tells her.

Raven takes the jacket and tries it on, an astonished look on her face. "Look, Talon," she says.

Talon nods as Mushom bends down to adjust the collar. "Your mom and your kohkum made this coat for you," Mushom tells her. "All year they worked on this. They knew you were coming to spend Christmas here." Raven admires the coat, stroking the leather and fur. Mushom finishes adjusting her collar and leans back to see how it fits. "Looks good," he says with a nod.

Raven nods too, beaming. She sits down at the table and holds her new coat close around her as she looks at the cabin walls. Talon and T-Bear have made their way to the table too and devour pieces of bannock.

"I hope everyone likes the decorations we made for Christmas," Raven says.

Mushom looks at the decorations and chucks Raven under the chin. "They're very nice, my girl," he tells her.

Talon and T-Bear each finish their pieces of bannock and reach for another, and Mushom nods towards the plate. "Have some bannock, my girl. We'll leave soon." Mushom grabs his fur cap and heads for the door as Raven turns and grabs a piece of bannock off the plate. When the door opens and the winter air hits the warmth of the cabin it creates steam that sweeps inside. The children see the dogs spring up. They bark and yelp in excitement as Mushom steps outside. When he closes the door behind him, the steam evaporates.

Raven turns to Talon. "What happens if we don't trap or hunt any food?" Talon has a mouthful of bannock so he can't answer right away, but T-Bear does.

"Then the family will have to split up. Some of you will go out to the trapline cabins for Christmas and some of us will have to go back to the city."

Raven looks at her brother and Talon nods, swallowing the bannock. "He's right."

"But the whole family is supposed to have Christmas together," Raven laments. The boys nod, but say nothing. They finish their bannock in silence before they get properly dressed for the outdoors. Each of them knows they'll be outside in the dead of winter for several hours. They've learned the importance of getting properly dressed.

Outside, Mushom places his duffel bag and his rifle in the sled, now sitting upright in the snow, while the children step outside and greet the dogs. T-Bear and Talon pet Shadow and Raven pets Freedom. "Good morning, Freedom," she says. Freedom stretches his neck out and she giggles and scratches it for him.

Mushom steps away from the sled and picks up a wooden sign that reads, "Checking traps again, will be back after sundown. Cyril." With a hammer he nails the sign to the door with one hard stroke. Raven continues to pet Freedom as the boys move over to the sled and poke through its contents.

"How old is Freedom?" Raven asks Mushom.

"Very old, but he knows this area better than any dog around," Mushom says with a smile. He chuckles as years of memories suddenly flash through his mind. "That dog and I have been through a lot together." He raises his voice a bit for the old dog. "You okay, Freedom?" Freedom barks and Mushom smiles. "Good." Raven moves over to Shadow, who wags his tail at her excitedly.

"Hey, Shadow," she says with a happy voice. "Do you want to go? You want to go?" Shadow yelps and wags his tail harder as she pets him on the head. "Yes, you do, don't you? How are you today?" His tail still wagging, Shadow relishes the attention and licks Raven's face in excitement. Raven laughs and wipes her face with her other mitten as she continues to pet Shadow. He turns still so she can pet him better, though his tail continues to wag. He almost looks as though he's smiling.

Raven gives him a curious look. "How old is Shadow?" she asks.

"He's young," Mushom tells her, "and strong. He'll make a good lead dog too someday. He picks up fast." Shadow suddenly stands in a ready position and stops wagging his tail, looking towards the lake. Raven, T-Bear, Talon, and Mushom also look towards the lake.

"Someone's coming," Mushom says.

"Can I take a look, Mushom?" T-Bear asks.

Mushom nods. "You know where they are."

T-Bear reaches into Mushom's duffel bag and digs around for a moment before he pulls out a pair of binoculars. He raises them to his eyes and adjusts the focus. Inside the magnified, circular view, T-Bear spots another dogsled moving swiftly across the frozen lake towards them. A man about the same age as Mushom drives the dog team.

"It's Uncle Peter!" T-Bear shouts. He lowers the binoculars and points in the direction of the approaching sled as Talon pulls them from his hands and peers through for his own look.

"With another body to help, we'll have a better chance," Mushom says with a smile.

Raven moves over and reaches for the binoculars too. "Can I see?" she asks her brother. Talon motions for her to wait for a moment as he watches Uncle Peter approach, his seven dogs charging hard. Talon smiles and passes the binoculars to his sister and she holds them to her eyes.

"Cool!" she says, seeing the image her brother and cousin saw before her, the dogs kicking up snow and snorting steam as they gallop across the lake. By now they can be seen clearly with the naked eye and Mushom watches Peter approach. The dogs all come to life as well, whining and barking greetings as Peter's team, led by a large black dog named Bear, closes the distance quickly, barking greetings of their own.

"Aiee!" Uncle Peter yells in the distance. Mushom and the children continue to watch them approach, the children impressed, Raven still following them with the binoculars.

"Uncle Peter's dogs are ever fast, eh Mushom?" Raven says, her eyes never leaving the approaching team.

Mushom chuckles. "Yeah, but they've got nothing on these dogs," he says, motioning to the excited group tied up beside them. Raven glances at Shadow and Freedom as they bark at the approaching team.

It doesn't take long for Uncle Peter's dog team to pull his sled off the lake and up the shore to the cabin, stopping in front of Mushom, T-Bear, Talon, Raven, and Mushom's team. Uncle Peter's dogs pant from the exertion and shake snow from their bodies as Uncle Peter plants the sled's foot brake. Mushom's dogs, with Freedom and Shadow out front, lean against the reins, keeping them in place, straining to sniff at Uncle Peter's dogs more closely. Uncle Peter's dogs bark at Mushom's dogs and Uncle Peter scowls at them.

"Ssshhht!" he utters. His dogs become quiet and Mushom's relax as Uncle Peter lowers his hood and steps over to Mushom and the children. He smiles and nods at Mushom and Mushom nods back. Peter turns to the children.

"Morning, Uncle Peter," the children all chime. Uncle Peter smiles and nods at them too.

"Morning," he says, then he turns back to Mushom. "Are we ready to go, *nistow*?"

Mushom turns from his brother-in-law and looks across the bay. He studies the horizon before he answers. "Eehee! The weather has been calm for too long now."

Peter also studies the horizon. "We need food for our families," he says. "And all I see is a beautiful day." They're all quiet for a moment, all studying the land and the sky. "We can stop at my cabin if we have to," Peter adds, then turns to the children. "Your auntie Anne will be waiting for us there with fresh bannock." The children all turn and look at Mushom, who finally nods.

The children yell cheerfully as they hop into their grandfather's sled and Uncle Peter walks back to his. Mushom is adjusting his mitts, when a raven caws and swoops down towards him. Mushom tries to duck, but the raven grabs his fur hat and flies back up into the tree. A few other hats lie perched on the branches around the jet-black bird. Uncle Peter and the children laugh as Mushom shakes his head.

"Iiee, I agree, Raven, the hunting is poor this year," he says as he leans into the sled. He reaches into the bag and pulls out another fur cap, identical to the one the raven just stole. He puts it on and stares up at the raven. "But you still have no need for all my hats." Uncle Peter and the children laugh again as Mushom, smiling now, steps around to the back of the sled and gets on.

"Two more days," Uncle Peter reminds everyone.

Mushom looks down into the smiling face of his granddaughter. "Raven?" he says.

Raven smiles and takes a deep breath as she faces Mushom's dog team. "Aiee!" she shouts in a commanding voice. Freedom barks and starts off with Shadow copying him. The other dogs follow suit and Mushom's sled speeds away from the cabin with the children inside.

Uncle Peter smiles as he watches them. "Aiee!" he shouts, and his dog team jumps into action after their short rest. Both dogsleds move down the slope and hiss onto the frozen lake.

"Aiee!" Mushom shouts.

"Aiee!" Peter shouts again.

The children hang on as the two dog teams move over the snow and ice. The sun now stretches above the horizon with three sundogs tagging along, one on top and two beside. The children notice them, each hoping and worrying at the same time.

CHAPTER TWO
Nets and Traps

The two dog teams continue to move across the lake, passing islands and inlets. T-Bear, Talon, and Raven watch the land go by from the comfort of Mushom's sled. The landmarks are becoming familiar to them now that they've spent time out here. Uncle Peter steers his dog team closer to Mushom's and waves to catch Mushom's attention. Mushom sees him and Uncle Peter points to the shore nearby. Mushom nods and both dog teams are steered towards land. The children watch as the two sleds reach shore and come to a stop, both Mushom and Uncle Peter hopping off.

"Why are we stopping?" T-Bear asks.

"We'll need some grass to cover the traps," Mushom tells them. The children climb out of the sled and Mushom and the boys grab three empty gunny sacks and walk to the dead grass by the shore.

"I'll continue on to the fishing hole," Uncle Peter tells them. "Anyone want to come along?"

"I do, Uncle," Raven yells. She hustles over to Uncle Peter's sled and hops in, then waves at her grandfather and her brother and cousin. "See you later."

"See you, sis," Talon yells.

"Have fun," Mushom calls out.

They give each other final waves as Uncle Peter gets back on the sled. "Aiee!" he yells and his dog team takes off. Mushom, Talon, and T-Bear watch them depart, hearing Raven start to pepper Uncle Peter with questions.

"Can we pick up Auntie Anne?" Raven asks in a loud voice.

"We'll see what she is doing," Uncle Peter responds.

As Uncle Peter's dog team pulls his sled further and further away, they can hear Raven ask more questions, but they can't make out the words. "Raven asks too many questions," T-Bear says.

Mushom chuckles and tells T-Bear that it's good to ask questions. "That's part of how you learn," he says. T-Bear shrugs as all three of them turn back to the shoreline and start to pick the grass, stuffing handfuls into the gunny sacks. They pull the tall, dead grass in silence, spreading out so they don't all pick in the same area. After a few minutes, Talon walks over to Mushom with his gunny sack and opens it.

"Is this enough, Mushom?" he asks.

Mushom looks inside the gunny sack and nods. "Yes, Talon, that should be fine, thank you."

T-Bear peers at the contents of Talon's gunny sack before Mushom closes it and lugs it back to the sled. T-Bear steps over to Talon and whispers, "A good hunter knows how much grass you need to cover the traps."

Talon gives T-Bear a scowl as T-Bear turns and picks one more handful of the dead grass. He stuffs it in his gunny sack and shows Talon. "Like that." T-Bear turns and heads over to the sled. Talon follows, his head hung low. Mushom watches them as T-Bear throws his gunny sack into the sled.

"Your great-grandfather used to take me through this trail many years ago," Mushom tells them. "There was lots of wildlife back then, but he only took two bullets with him. That was all he needed. One bullet was for a moose or a caribou, and another for a ptarmigan."

T-Bear gives his mushom a smug look. "I would take a lot of bullets so I wouldn't have to hunt all season," he says. "Just get as much as I could in a couple of days."

Mushom and Talon share a look, then Mushom chuckles. "That might seem like the easier way to do it," he says to T-Bear, "but if you took all the big animals, you would not be able to hunt in that area for a long time. What you do to one animal affects them all, including yourself."

T-Bear thinks about that as Mushom and Talon get the sled ready to go. Talon and T-Bear climb in as

Mushom releases the foot brake. "Aiee!" he yells, and Freedom and Shadow let out barks as they press forward, letting the other dogs know it's time to go. The other dogs bark back and the dog team pulls the sled out onto the lake. The two boys and their Mushom are quiet as T-Bear continues to mull over his mushom's words, the hissing of the sled gliding over the ice and snow filling their ears.

UNCLE PETER drives his dog team towards shore, where his log cabin sits among the trees, smoke billowing from its chimney. Raven sits in the sled, her eyes squinting from the spray of snow the dogs kick up, but with a big smile on her face. She points to shore where an elderly woman stands outside the cabin. They're close enough now for her to make out who it is.

"There's Aunt Anne!" she says excitedly. In truth, Uncle Peter and Aunt Anne are Raven's great-uncle and great-aunt, but the children, and everyone else under the age of fifty, call them aunt and uncle.

Raven waves at the figure on shore and Aunt Anne waves back. Uncle Peter steers the dogs towards a trail cut into the shoreline. It leads them right to the cabin, where they come to a stop.

"Hi, Auntie!" Raven says. Aunt Anne smiles at Raven, who climbs out of the sled as Uncle Peter steps on the foot brake.

"Hi, my girl," Aunt Anne says to Raven. "Where's your mushom? Is something wrong?" Raven gives Aunt Anne a big hug.

"He's fine," Uncle Peter tells his wife. "They're all fine. They're just checking the traps over by Eagle Point." He walks over to Aunt Anne and kisses her. She looks at him with concern.

"I'm just worried about Cyril," she says. "He's getting old. I keep telling him to slow down. I tell him, 'You're not a spring chicken, you know. You cannot keep trapping like there's no tomorrow.'"

Raven looks at Aunt Anne with some worry. Uncle Peter sees her reaction and grabs a duffel bag out of the sled. He passes it to Raven. "Can you put this inside the cabin?"

"Sure," Raven says, taking the duffel bag. "Be right back."

Raven steps over to the cabin. When she slips inside, Uncle Peter turns to Aunt Anne.

"Trapping is the only thing that occupies him out here," he tells her. "Ever since Jacob moved to the city, Cyril and Rosalie continue to maintain their trapline. Sitting in a retirement home in town is not their way."

Aunt Anne nods. "It is good to see Jacob's son helping Mushom out and learning."

Uncle Peter and Aunt Anne haven't heard Raven step back outside. She stands there, an indignant look on her face.

"Mushom doesn't need any help," she says. Uncle Peter and Aunt Anne both turn and look at her. "He is strong," Raven adds. "He carried..." she tries to remember, but can't, so she raises her arms to show that it was a big load and guesses, "...a thousand kilograms of flour on his back two years ago at the Winter Festival when he won first prize in the trapper contest."

"Yes, he did," Uncle Peter says, hiding a smile.

"And you're right," Aunt Anne adds. "No one has to help your mushom." Raven nods and leaves it at that. Uncle Peter turns to his wife.

"Raven was wondering if you would like to come with us to check the nets," he tells her. Aunt Anne looks at Raven and smiles.

"Can you, Auntie?" Raven pleads. "You don't have to be a spring chicken to check the nets. It's easy."

Aunt Anne laughs. "Let me grab my knitting and we will go," she says.

"Yay!" Raven cheers. She hops back into the sled as Aunt Anne enters the cabin.

FREEDOM, SHADOW, AND THE OTHER DOGS stand guard in front of the sled as Mushom, T-Bear, and Talon hike towards the bush, all of them wearing snowshoes. The boys are having a bit of trouble and Mushom smiles at them.

"This is how your great-grandfather hunted years ago, before dog teams," he tells them. The boys listen with respect. "Today young people get upset that they have to haul their own gas on their snowmobiles. Ha!" He shakes his head. "That's not work. Walking back through deep snow while the dogs hauled the meat in the sled, now that builds character. We never complained. If you wanted to eat, you had to do the work."

The boys nod as they move forward, the soft crackling of their snowshoes the only sound they hear. Mushom slows down as he nears a stand of bushes.

"Here are my traps," he announces. The boys nod again, both remembering, though Talon more so. All three stop for a moment, each hoping they find something in the traps. Mushom points to a spot several metres away. "T-Bear, Talon, you two check the trap over there," he tells them. "I'll check this other one."

T-Bear and Talon look at each other and smile. "See that short pine tree?" T-Bear asks, pointing to a tree about five metres from the spot Mushom pointed at. Talon nods. "I'll get there first!" T-Bear blurts, taking off. Talon is fast on his heels.

"No you won't!" Talon yells.

The two boys hustle through the snow as fast as their snowshoes will allow. Mushom watches them for a moment, then chuckles when he realizes their horsing around won't take them near the trap he sent them to check. He starts for the other trap. As the boys continue their race, Mushom reaches the trap and drops to his knees. He parts the bushes and brushes away snow to reveal the trap – the empty trap. Seeing that it's empty, Mushom lowers his head and lets out a sigh.

Talon has caught up to T-Bear and they bump into each other, causing Talon to fall into the snow. T-Bear reaches the trap first. "I beat you! I beat you!" he yells in celebration.

"Not fair!" Talon yells, pulling himself up from the snow. "You had a head start and you pushed me."

"It was an accident," T-Bear says.

Mushom watches them for a moment, then bends over and grabs his side in pain. He lets out a quiet groan as Talon, covered in snow, follows T-Bear over to some bushes. Talon parts the branches and brushes away some snow to reveal the second trap. Like the first, the trap is empty.

"Nothing," Talon says as T-Bear peers around him for a look.

"It's empty!" Talon shouts to Mushom. He turns to see where Mushom is and sees him kneeling in the snow with his hands on his side. "Mushom?" he yells. "Are you okay?"

T-Bear turns and sees Mushom too. "I think he's praying," he says.

With his back turned to the boys, Mushom's expression of pain fades and he gets to his feet. "I'm okay, boys," he tells them. "This trap is empty too. We better move to the next spot."

As Mushom starts for the sled, Talon looks at T-Bear with concern and T-Bear shrugs. "He said he's okay," T-Bear whispers. Talon nods, but he looks unconvinced. The boys trot over to Mushom and walk with him back to the sled, where the dogs wait, their tails wagging as the three trappers approach.

CHAPTER THREE
Burnt Trees and the Deer

On another part of the lake, Uncle Peter chops through the thin ice that has formed over an ice hole, as Raven and Aunt Anne sit on the sled. Raven watches Uncle Peter for a moment, hoping, wishing, and praying he finds a lot of fish in the net beneath the ice. She looks over at Aunt Anne, who sews beads on a pair of mukluks, trying to see if she's worried or not. If Aunt Anne is worried, she doesn't show it, focusing instead on the beads and the mukluks. Raven looks down at the partially finished leather pouch sitting in her lap, the needle and thread in her hand. She takes another look at Uncle Peter, now pulling the net from the hole in the ice, and resumes her own sewing. Aunt Anne glances at her and smiles.

"I remember when I used to show your mom how to make her own clothes for winter, when she was your age," Aunt Anne says. Raven shifts closer to her aunt. "She would sew for hours," Aunt Anne continues, then points at Raven's new coat. "She made that for you."

Raven smiles and pulls the coat tighter around her body. "It's warm," she says, then holds up the pouch. "This is for Mushom."

Aunt Anne studies the pouch and nods. "That's good work. Your Mushom will like it."

Raven smiles hard and takes a blanket from the bottom of the sled. She wraps it around Aunt Anne's legs. Aunt Anne smiles back at her. "Thank you, my girl."

"You're welcome," Raven says. They both resume their sewing as Uncle Peter continues to haul the long net from beneath the ice. "Auntie Anne?" Raven asks a few moments later.

"Uh-huh?"

"Are you hungry?"

Aunt Anne smiles and rubs Raven's back. "Have some more bannock, my girl." Raven nods and puts her sewing aside as she digs into one of the bags in the sled. Aunt Anne looks over towards Peter, concern finally showing on her face. Uncle Peter has finished pulling the long net from beneath the ice and gathers the few fish the net caught.

"How many?" Aunt Anne calls out. Raven looks up, chewing her first bite of bannock, and waits for Uncle

Peter to answer. Uncle Peter drops the last of the fish onto the ice.

"Four," Uncle Peter shouts back. With that Aunt Anne turns back to her sewing, hiding her concern. Raven studies her for a moment before she climbs out of the sled and trots after Uncle Peter, who makes his way to the other ice hole.

"The fire affected the number of fish too," Uncle Peter tells Raven as she catches up him. "We barely have enough to feed the dogs."

"What did the fire do to the fish?" Raven asks.

"It made ash that got swept into the lake," Uncle Peter says, "and it made the water too warm. Lot of fish died, like they were cooked."

Raven's heart sinks, but she tries to keep a positive attitude for her Uncle Peter's benefit. "Don't worry, Uncle," she tells him, "not all the fish got cooked. Where there's four, there's more."

Uncle Peter smiles at her. "I hope so, Raven... I sure hope so."

Raven watches as Uncle Peter drops to his knees, pulls out his hatchet, and starts to chop through the thin ice covering the second ice hole. Once he reaches fresh water, he puts the hatchet down and starts to pull the net from beneath the ice. "Wanna help me?" he asks Raven. Without answering, Raven steps forward and grabs hold of the net with her warm mitts and helps Uncle Peter pull it from the water.

MUSHOM DRIVES the dogsled along a trail through the forest, Freedom at the front with Shadow at second, and the rest of the dogs in behind. Talon and T-Bear sit in the sled, T-Bear staring ahead, watching the dogs. Talon watches and studies the land around them, looking for tracks. So does Mushom.

"Many times my father and I had a moose or a caribou within range," Mushom tells the boys, "only to have your great-grandfather drop it with one shot." He laughs and coughs loudly. Talon turns and looks at him with concern and sees the old man smiling as he recovers.

"I said to him, 'You could've given me a chance to shoot at least once, Dad.' Then he said to me, 'You only need one shot, my boy. There will be many more days and many more animals around here for you, my son.'"

Talon continues to study his grandfather. "Are there more animals now, Mushom?" he asks. Mushom takes awhile to answer, remembering the summer before.

"No, my boy, the fire made sure of that."

Talon studies his grandfather for another moment before he turns back to the land and searches for tracks, the need still great, but the likelihood becoming less and less. Seeing Talon look suddenly more serious, T-Bear turns and looks at Mushom. Mushom smiles at him and urges the dogs on.

"Aiee!"

And Freedom leads the dog team further along the trail towards the lake. They all look up as the sled descends from land to shore, bobbing over the terrain, emerging from forest trees, across piled-up ice, and onto the bay. Mushom pulls the dog team to a stop on the ice and the boys stare across the frozen water to the far mainland, not believing what they see – burnt trees to the horizon.

"Is that from the fire?" T-Bear asks. Mushom nods. Talon shakes his head. Of course, he thinks to himself, what else would it be from? They stare at the sight before them, T-Bear with wonder, Talon and Mushom with renewed concern.

"Will the animals come back?" Talon asks. T-Bear turns and looks at Mushom for the answer. Mushom stares solemnly at the stark reminder before him.

"It'll be awhile," he says, "but let's see what is still around."

Mushom tugs on the reins and Freedom leads the dogs forward, T-Bear and Talon grabbing the sides of the sled for support. The sled moves steadily across the bay as Mushom, Talon, and T-Bear continue to stare at the amazing amount of damage left by the fire. Eventually Freedom leads them to the far shore and they bounce off the lake and back onto land. Mushom urges the dogs on and they lean up into the forest and accelerate down another trail.

"We'll stop to eat and have some tea up ahead," Mushom tells the boys. T-Bear nods, his stomach rumbling from hunger.

Talon's stomach is growling too, but he knows they can't afford to stop for too long. By now they have less than two days to get enough food for the whole family to stay for Christmas, and the more they search, the more it becomes clear that there's hardly any food around. And yet he knows they have to eat, to keep up enough energy to stay on the trail.

And as these thoughts go through his mind, his respect for his mushom deepens. To do this your whole life, Talon thinks to himself, and be that good at it. Only now, after the fire, is there the chance that the whole family won't be together at Christmas, for the first time in his life — maybe for the first time in all their lives.

Mushom pulls the reins and Freedom stops, with Shadow following suit. The other dogs follow their cue and the sled runners crunch to a halt on the hard-packed snow of the trail.

"We'll stop here," Mushom says, forcing the foot brake deep into the snow. Talon and T-Bear climb out of the sled as Mushom steps forward and unties the dogs. He takes their lines and ties them to a stake he drives hard into the snow. Freedom walks up to Mushom and wags his tail and the old man pats the old dog on the back before he returns to the sled. Freedom lies down to rest. The other dogs do the same, except for Shadow, whose youthful energy keeps him sitting alert and watching the humans.

"You boys gather some wood," Mushom says. The boys immediately do as they are told, moving off into the bush. Mushom watches them for a moment, then lets out a long breath as he turns and grabs his duffel bag from the sled and places it on the ground. Untying it, he reaches in and pulls out some dried meat and steps over to the dogs. Shadow wags his tail immediately as Mushom tosses several chunks of the meat on the snow beside him. With two quick bites, Shadow has two large pieces of the meat in his mouth and he turns and lies in the snow, curling up to protect his food. The other dogs catch the scent of meat and stir to life, all nipping at various bits of the food.

Only Freedom keeps from the fray. Mushom steps over to the lead dog. He squats beside him and gives Freedom a pat on the head. Tired, Freedom wags his tail and Mushom holds out a large chunk of dried meat. "Here you go, boy." Freedom leans forward and bares his teeth before gently snatching the meat from Mushom's fingers. Mushom chuckles as he watches Freedom savour his meal. "That's a boy," Mushom says.

A branch snaps in the distance and Mushom looks off in the direction the boys went before he moves back towards the sled.

In the trees, Talon and T-Bear each carry an armful of branches and small boughs. "I think we have enough," T-Bear suggests.

Talon's not so sure. "We don't want to run out," he says.

T-Bear shakes his head and turns back towards the shore. "Mushom's making tea," he mutters, "we aren't preparing a feast."

Talon watches his cousin move through the dense bush with his load of firewood, looking annoyed. Talon smiles and shakes his head. "Okay," he calls out. T-Bear keeps walking through the dense bush without looking back. Still smiling, Talon trots after him with his own load of firewood.

When the boys emerge from the trees into the clearing where Mushom waits by the sled, he turns and smiles at them. "Who wants to build the fire?" he asks. T-Bear looks hesitant.

Talon waits, looking at his cousin, but when it becomes obvious that T-Bear isn't going to say anything, Talon steps forward. "I will," he announces. Mushom nods and hands Talon the box of matches and some dried bark.

Talon sets his load of firewood on the ground and takes the matches and bark. He drops to his knees and starts to arrange the branches, placing the bark in the middle. T-Bear finally steps forward and adds his load to the pile and Talon uses them to complete the configuration.

T-Bear watches his cousin work. He doesn't know how to start a fire and he knows Talon knows that. But T-Bear wants to learn, so he stays to watch, knowing that Talon knows he's there. Talon turns and looks at him and T-Bear shrugs. Talon turns back to the structure he's built and T-Bear lets out a breath. By his little shrug he's just admitted that Talon is winning. Talon knows more about taking care of himself out on the land than T-Bear. But admitting it shows T-Bear wants to learn, and that's something Talon knows as well.

Talon takes another glance at T-Bear before he huddles over the carefully piled branches and reaches through to the dried bark in the centre with both hands, a wooden match in the right and the box in the left. T-Bear watches closely and Mushom smiles and watches them both.

Talon strikes the match against the box and the tip ignites into a small flame. Quickly but carefully, he places the match tip in with the finer, shredded bits of bark in the centre of the dried bark pile. The shreds catch fire and spread the flames to the other pieces of bark as Talon gently blows at them, fuelling the small blaze. Talon nurtures it and soon the entire bark pile burns, its flames licking at the dried branches, the smaller and medium-size ones already catching fire. Talon leans back to admire his handiwork as Mushom nods.

"Good work, my boy," he says. Talon glows in the praise. T-Bear concentrates, trying to remember everything Talon did.

Soon the campfire crackles as strong gusts of wind blow furiously through the area. A particularly strong one knocks Mushom's hat off. Mushom grabs for it, but the wind is quick and his hat evades his reach and lands in the deep snow several metres away. Talon and T-Bear try not to smile as Mushom shakes his head and looks up at the bright blue sky.

"Iiee," Mushom begins. "Grandfathers, if you allow us a safe journey so we can finish our day's tasks, I will be grateful. *Tenigi!*"

Both boys get up to go after their mushom's hat, but T-Bear gets a head start and Talon lets him go. T-Bear grabs the hat and returns, when they hear a loud groaning in the distance, causing both of them to jump. Mushom tries to hide the fact that he's chuckling, but both boys see right through it. Talon is annoyed with himself. T-Bear is less so.

"Are you afraid to be out here by yourself?" T-Bear asks his mushom.

Mushom chuckles out loud and looks at T-Bear. "Why would I be afraid on my own land?"

T-Bear shrugs. "All these noises," he says.

"That was a tree bending in the wind," Mushom tells him.

Talon hides his smile as T-Bear turns and stares into the fire. They're all quiet for awhile as Talon builds up the blaze by adding more wood. "Are we going to eat?" T-Bear finally asks. Mushom pulls out three more hunks of dried meat from his duffel bag and passes two to the boys.

"I had to give the rest to the dogs so they can get us home," Mushom says. "I thought we would have found something else for them by now." The boys bite into their portions of dried meat, both satisfied with Mushom's logic and just happy to have something to eat. Mushom gnaws on his piece of dried meat as he pulls a black pot from his duffel bag.

"Talon," Mushom says. Talon and T-Bear both look up. Mushom keeps his eyes on Talon. "Let's get some water from the creek." Talon nods and stands up as Mushom turns to T-Bear. "You watch the fire." T-Bear nods as Talon and Mushom stride off.

T-Bear turns back to the fire and, seeing that it's raging pretty good, he kneels beside Freedom. "How you doing, boy?" he asks. Freedom licks T-Bear in the face in response.

Talon and Mushom venture carefully down the shore's embankment, stepping on rocks and outcroppings for support and leverage. "Be careful," Mushom says, watching his feet closely, "it's slippery."

Further down, Talon turns and gives his mushom a look before he slides the last few feet of the bank to the water. The creek is swift so it hasn't frozen through. Talon dips the black pot into the ice-cold water until it's full and pulls it back out of the stream. "Got it," he tells his mushom.

Mushom reaches down and Talon passes him the black pot, heavy with its load. With the pot in hand,

Mushom climbs back up the embankment. Free of the heavy load, Talon clambers up after him. As they continue up, Mushom's foot suddenly slips out from under him and he slides back down to the creek, taking Talon with him.

"Whoa!" they both wail. Mushom lifts the pot above his head and Talon helps him hold it there as they come to a stop. With the pot of water safe, Talon smiles at his mushom.

"Not a drop spilled!" he yells.

Mushom chuckles, then a twig snaps across the stream. Mushom and Talon both turn and see a young deer jump out of the trees. Mushom grabs Talon's arm and motions for him to be quiet and absolutely still. Silently, they watch as the deer takes a long look around, scanning the clearing. It doesn't see them, even though it's only about twenty metres away. The deer takes a step forward and stops to hear his own hoof crack through the snow. After a few more slow steps, the deer crosses the creek to the other side. It turns to a patch of wild grass sticking out of the snow and starts eating. Mushom motions to Talon and they make their way back up the slope.

As Mushom and Talon return to the sled, Mushom puts his finger to his lips to tell T-Bear to be quiet, then motions for him to stay here. T-Bear nods as Talon gently places the pot of water on the fire. Mushom grabs his rifle from his sled and places shells in his pocket.

T-Bear looks puzzled as Mushom and Talon quickly but quietly run from the camp, but it only takes him a moment to realize they must have seen an animal.

As he watches his cousin and his mushom step quietly down the bank, T-Bear suddenly knows that with one shot all their problems will be over.

CHAPTER FOUR
The Island

Mushom and Talon move slowly and silently through the deep snow on the other side of the creek before Mushom motions for them to stop. Talon searches through the trees, but can't see the deer. Mushom listens and they both hear a rustling in the distance. Mushom leans over to Talon and whispers, "It's still walking. It can't hear us."

As Talon remains still, Mushom looks back at T-Bear standing by the campfire. He waves at T-Bear then points at him and the dogs and indicates they're to come over, but putting his fingers to his lips, he shows that he means it to be done quietly.

At least that's what T-Bear thinks he means. As he watches Mushom turn back to the trees, T-Bear looks over at Freedom. "We have to be quiet, boy," he whispers as he moves towards the dogs. He thinks it through carefully, how to get the dogs and the sled back together and not only ready to go, but leading them down towards Mushom and Talon, and quietly, so he won't scare away whatever it is they're chasing. Above all, he knows how important it is that he get it right. He lets out a quick sigh and unties the lead rein from the wooden stake Mushom stuck deep into the snow.

"Help me out here, boy," T-Bear whispers to Freedom. The old dog gets to his feet and Shadow and the others do the same.

T-Bear takes them over to the sled and secures the main line to the front end while Talon and Mushom move further along the shore in the deep snow, still quiet, still alert. Mushom stops again and Talon does the same. Together they listen, but the sound of rustling branches in the distance has stopped. Mushom looks at Talon and Talon shakes his head. Mushom scans the trees as Talon looks down the shoreline and out over the lake.

And that's when he sees the deer, out on the snow-covered ice near the bottom of a hill. Talon quickly waves at Mushom to catch his attention, then points at the deer. Mushom nods, and moves quietly up towards a rocky ledge where he can get a better view, and a better shot. Figuring that out, Talon follows. When they reach the ledge, Mushom ignores the pain in his side and gets down on his stomach, with Talon sliding in beside him. A hundred metres away, they see the deer crossing the lake towards an island.

Mushom calmly cocks the rifle and takes aim. He's able to hold the barrel steady, but he has to squint and blink hard to make out the deer in the distance, straining to change the blur into something clear. Giving up, he aims at the spot where the blurry deer's heart should be and squeezes the trigger. Talon covers his ears as the shot rips into the air, with a deafening crack that echoes out across the land before the sound slowly fades and disappears. The deer jumps and quickens its pace to reach the island. Mushom shakes his head. Talon can't believe it.

"My eyesight is not as good as it used to be," Mushom sadly admits.

The sound of the dogs and the runners of the sled gliding across the snow catch Mushom and Talon's attention. They turn and hustle down towards T-Bear and the dog team.

"What is it? What are you shooting at?" T-Bear asks as he pulls the dogs to a stop.

"A deer," Talon says as he quickly jumps into the sled. T-Bear passes the reins to Mushom and jumps in the sled as well. Mushom hops astride the runners.

"Aiee!" The dog team starts off again, pushing hard and fast as they leave the shoreline and accelerate onto the lake towards the island.

"Where is it?" T-Bear asks as he scans the lake.

"On the island," Mushom says. "He'll either stay there and take cover, or try and get to the other side and make it across the rest of the lake." The boys take this in and they're all quiet for a moment as Freedom leads the other dogs hard across the lake, the wind stinging T-Bear and Talon on the cheeks.

"Do you think we'll get him?" T-Bear asks, breaking the silence.

"We're sure gonna try," Mushom says. They turn quiet again as they reach the island. At two hundred metres across, it is large enough to hide a deer, but small enough for a dog team to haul a sled around it in a few minutes. It takes Freedom and the rest of Mushom's dog team only two as they circle back to the tracks the deer made going in.

"Did it cross to the other side of the lake yet, Mushom?" T-Bear asks.

"No, T-Bear," Mushom says, pointing to the tracks. "The deer came in this way but there weren't any other tracks to show that he came out."

As the huskies continue their gallop over the deep snow, Mushom pulls on their lines to slow them down. "Whoa!" He steers them in a wide turn back around to the deer tracks. The dogs ease their pace as Mushom keeps watch, scanning the treeline.

"So the deer is still on the island," Talon says. Mushom nods as he brings the dogs to a stop. The boys see the deer tracks lead up to the bush, where they disappear. They study the trees, trying to search through them as Mushom steps on the foot brake, forcing it deep into the snow. He steps off the sled and doubles over as a sharp pain shoots through his body. The boys have their backs to him, so they don't see it. Mushom struggles to stand up straight and puts on a brave face. He takes his rifle out of the sled and, clutching his right side, walks towards the trees.

"You see it, Mushom?" T-Bear asks. Mushom gestures for the boys to be silent as he moves further away from the sled. The blinding glare of the sun reflected off the snow makes it difficult for Mushom to see through the dense bush of the island. He turns to the boys, motions for them to get out and walk towards the island. The boys don't react right away, not sure what Mushom wants them to do.

"Does he want us to scare the deer out into the open?" T-Bear asks his younger cousin.

Talon shakes his head. "I'm not sure."

The boys climb out of the sled and slowly approach the island as Talon looks at Mushom still moving in the other direction. "There's something wrong," Talon says, motioning to Mushom. "He's holding his side."

T-Bear studies Mushom, who cuts a new trail through the deep snow. "He looks fine to me," T-Bear says. He turns back and hustles onto the island with Talon right behind him. Cutting a new trail of their own through the deep snow, the boys trudge up to the treeline where the deer tracks disappear.

"Now?" T-Bear asks. Talon shrugs. Both boys reach up and grab large branches from the trees closest to them. They begin shaking the branches hard, the loud rustling shattering the silence. The deer suddenly leaps out of the bushes and races out onto the lake in front of Mushom and sprints towards the mainland. Mushom kneels in the snow, raises his rifle and takes aim. The deer races farther and farther away as Mushom struggles to focus his eyes.

"Shoot!" T-Bear yells, urging Mushom on. Talon watches, hoping.

The deer rambles off the lake and onto the mainland before it disappears into the forest. Mushom lowers his rifle in defeat. "Aiee," he mutters to himself. He sits on the ice and holds his side again. The boys make their way back to the sled and bring it over to Mushom. Freedom nudges Mushom with his nose and Mushom manages a smile and pets the dog as the boys make their way over.

"What happened?" T-Bear asks. "Why didn't you shoot?"

Mushom sighs and looks at the two boys standing above him. "There is a reason the Creator sent you boys here. Your mushom is getting too old for this now."

T-Bear looks at Talon with concern. Talon manages to hide his. "Don't worry, Mushom. We'll find enough food for Christmas," Talon says. "A good hunter is never stuck."

Mushom smiles and gets to his feet. "You're good boys," he tells them.

The boys hold their Mushom's hands as they move back to the sled. Talon looks up at Mushom and smiles, and Mushom smiles back, but when they look away, their smiles are replaced with looks of concern.

CHAPTER FIVE
More Tracks

Uncle Peter stands on the runners of the dogsled as it moves quickly over the frozen lake towards Mushom's cabin, Bear leading the rest of Uncle Peter's dog team. Aunt Anne and Raven ride in the sled and crane their necks when they see a group of people waiting for them on shore.

"I think your parents have arrived," Aunt Anne tells Raven. Raven smiles hard, trying to see through the snow kicked up by Uncle Peter's dog team. On the shore she can make out a grey canvas trapline tent with its own chimney, set up close to the cabin.

"Do you think we'll all get to spend Christmas together, Auntie Anne?" Raven asks.

Aunt Anne pats Raven on the knee. "I hope so, my girl," she says. "I hope so."

Uncle Peter urges his dogs on as the people on shore all turn and face the approaching sled. Standing out front is Mushom's wife, Kohkum Rosalie. Behind her stand Raven and Talon's parents, Sarah and Alphonse. Sarah is Mushom and Kohkum's daughter and Alphonse is a Dene man from further north. Beside them is T-Bear's dad, Jacob – Mushom's only son. They all start waving as the sled draws near. Aunt Anne and Raven wave back as Uncle Peter steers the dog team off the lake and up the shore. They come to a stop in front of the group and Raven races out of the sled.

"Mom! Dad!" she yells, and she races into her mother's arms. Sarah hugs her girl as Alphonse joins them. "I missed you," Raven says.

"I missed you too," Sarah replies. Raven turns to Alphonse and gives him a hug as well. Alphonse lifts her up and gives her a kiss before placing her back down on the ground. The others watch the family reunion, smiling at the sweetness of the moment.

Raven turns away from her dad and hugs Kohkum Rosalie. "I missed you too, Kohkum," she says. Kohkum lets out a loud chuckle and hugs her back before Raven squirms free and displays her new coat. "Look! I'm wearing the new coat you and Mom made for me."

"I see," Kohkum Rosalie says, checking to make sure the coat fits properly.

"It fits fine," Raven tells her. "I love it." And she hugs her Kohkum again.

"Ah, you're a sweet girl, Raven. So much love to spread around," Kohkum Rosalie says as she hugs Raven back. Jacob, Sarah, and Alphonse turn to Uncle Peter and Aunt Anne.

"Where are Dad and the boys?" Jacob asks.

Uncle Peter motions across the lake, pointing with his lips. "They're still checking the traps." Sarah and Alphonse nod, but Jacob seems concerned as he looks out across the lake. "That T-Bear is going to be a good trapper," Uncle Peter continues. "He might even take over his mushom's trapline some day."

Aunt Anne and Kohkum Rosalie each give Uncle Peter a dour look – the kind you give someone when you know they're deliberately trying to get under someone else's skin. As Raven steps over to her mother again, and takes her by the hand, Jacob looks at Uncle Peter with some fire in his eyes. It's clear Uncle Peter did get under his skin, because Jacob is mad, but he takes a breath to keep it under control. Uncle Peter, after all, is his elder.

"Not everyone is meant to spend their life on the trapline, Uncle Peter," Jacob finally manages to say. He says it with a smile, but everyone knows he is not happy. Everyone, that is, except Raven, who is just glad to be with her parents again – not to mention the rest of the family, the family she hopes will get to spend Christmas together.

Uncle Peter grabs a fishing auger – used to cut holes in the ice – out of the sled and looks Jacob in the eye.

"Some of us are," he says politely.

Jacob wants to respond, but holds his tongue, afraid what might come out of his mouth.

Auntie Anne coughs on purpose to relieve the tension. She hits Uncle Peter in the arm and motions to the back of the cabin. "Go put that away," she tells her husband. Uncle Peter and Jacob hold eye contact for another moment before Uncle Peter goes off to do what his wife said. Jacob turns and looks at Alphonse, who shrugs sympathetically.

Aunt Anne turns to Kohkum Rosalie. "How was your trip to the city?" They share a hug in the way that sisters do.

"It was too busy," Kohkum Rosalie complains over Aunt Anne's shoulder, "everybody rushing this way and that way. If it weren't for Alphonse and Sarah, nobody would've said hello or anything to me."

They end their hug and Aunt Anne nods knowingly. "It is a different world," she says.

"I'm just glad to be back," Kohkum Rosalie replies.

"Mom, it's not that bad," Jacob pipes in before he remembers his manners, realizing he forgot to greet his aunt. "Hi, Aunt Anne," he says with a smile. "It's good to see you." He leans in and kisses her on the cheek.

"You too, my boy," Aunt Anne says. "And don't mind your uncle. You know what's best for T-Bear."

"I know," Jacob says. "And I know Uncle Peter means well, but he has to understand that my life and T-Bear's life don't revolve around living on the land."

"He knows," Kohkum Rosalie speaks up, "and so does your father. They just want someone to take over the traplines when they're gone."

"Someone will," Jacob says, "it just won't be me...or T-Bear."

"Me and Talon can do it," Raven blurts out. The adults are surprised for a moment, then they all laugh warmly. Kohkum steps over and takes Raven's hand.

"I'm sure you can, my girl," Kohkum says, "I'm sure you can. Now let's get you inside so you can warm up." She hands Raven over to Sarah as everyone turns and heads for the cabin.

As Jacob passes Kohkum Rosalie, she grabs him by the arm, forcing him to stop. "And you should talk to your father," she tells him quietly. Jacob nods respectfully and Kohkum Rosalie moves off, following the others.

"I helped Uncle Peter pull the fishnet from under the ice," Raven tells her mother.

"Did you?" Sarah responds.

"Uh-huh."

The adults smile again at Raven, who reaches the door first. She scoots inside as the adults follow. Jacob is the last to enter. He turns before going in as Uncle Peter comes around from behind the cabin. They look at each other again before Jacob steps inside. Uncle Peter lets out a long sigh as he walks up to the front door.

BACK ON ANOTHER PART OF THE LAKE, Talon and T-Bear begin to pull a fishing net from a different ice hole than those checked by Uncle Peter, Raven, and Aunt Anne. Mushom rests by the sled, watching the boys huff and puff and pull on the net with all their might as it slowly inches from the frozen lake.

"Hopefully we'll eat some fish tonight," Mushom says in a loud, encouraging voice.

The boys stay focused on the task at hand, but T-Bear looks rather indignant. "He was so close," he says quietly to Talon. "I could have shot that deer."

"No, you couldn't," Talon quietly replies. "You've never shot a real animal, only tin cans and bottles."

"Yeah, but I hit them every time – nothing to it," T-Bear finishes, still in a hushed voice. T-Bear and Talon think they are speaking quietly enough so that Mushom can't hear them. Truth is, Mushom's eyesight may be going, but his hearing is just fine. He gets up and walks over to the boys as they continue to struggle with the net.

"There is always something more to learn and do when you live off this land," Mushom tells them. "That is what your great-grandfather said to me when I used to think I knew it all."

T-Bear gives Mushom a guilty look. Talon keeps his eyes on the net as they manage to pull its entire length from the lake. They lay it out on the ice and search for fish, but it becomes very clear that the net is empty.

"Nothing!" T-Bear laments. The three of them just stand there, staring at the empty net in silence. Behind them, Shadow whimpers.

Mushom finally lets out a breath. "Time to head back to the cabin," he says, trying to hide his dismay. He turns and saunters back to the sled and the boys both follow, all of them looking very weary and concerned. They each try not to show it, but the same thought runs through their minds – only one more day to catch enough food to feed the family for Christmas. If not, everyone will have to leave.

The boys climb into the sled as Mushom gingerly steps on the runners at the back. He releases the foot brake and lets out a breath. "Aiee!" he shouts at the dogs. Freedom barks and leads the rest of the dog team across the frozen lake towards Mushom's cabin. T-Bear and Talon huddle in the sled, trying to stay warm. Mushom grimaces, still in some pain, but the boys keep their eyes forward and don't notice. All of them are silent for several minutes on the first part of the ride.

Eventually Talon looks to the sky where clouds have begun to move in. He closes his eyes and very quietly whispers to himself in prayer. "Grandfathers, please help our family this Christmas. Our traps are empty and the fish are gone. We need your help." He stops there for a moment before he adds, "If you can hear me, please show us a sign. *Tenigi!*"

Talon opens his eyes expectantly, but the skis on the sled gliding over the ice and snow and the dogs running are the only sounds he can hear. He lowers his head sadly as T-Bear looks at him. Mushom, meanwhile, has been keeping his eyes on the ice and snow, searching. And then something catches his eye.

"Whoa!" Mushom yells, pulling on the lines. The dogs stop abruptly and the boys pitch forward. When they regain their balance, they turn and look at Mushom with surprise. When the sled comes to a complete stop, Mushom drives the foot brake deep into the snow and hops off the runners. He trots back along the trail, the pain in his side forgotten for the moment. Talon and T-Bear both stand up.

"What is it, Mushom?" T-Bear calls out.

"Moose tracks!" Mushom yells back.

Talon looks up at the sky and smiles at the clouds. T-Bear hops out of the sled and races after Mushom. Talon climbs out of the sled as well. He runs over and joins Mushom and T-Bear, who have both stopped to examine the moose tracks, Mushom down on one knee. Talon steps up behind them and has a look.

"They're new," Mushom says. The tracks are also big and Talon sees them lead off into the distance towards another island. Mushom and T-Bear stare at the island too.

"Can we get it?" T-Bear asks.

Mushom looks at the sky and shakes his head. "It's getting dark," he says. He turns back to the boys and sees the disappointed looks on their faces. "Don't worry, he won't go far. We'll track him tomorrow."

Talon nods first, then T-Bear. Mushom turns and starts back towards the sled as the boys fall in beside him.

"Think it's a big one?" T-Bear asks.

Mushom nods. "Looks like it might be big enough to feed the whole family for awhile. But let's not say anything about it when we get back. I don't want to get everyone's hopes up."

Talon and T-Bear nod, liking what they hear, but looks of concern spread across their faces as Mushom starts to favour his side again, limping slightly. Talon and T-Bear share a look as Mushom gingerly gets on the back of the sled. He looks up at the snow clouds stretching across the sky towards them. "Hurry up, my grandchildren. It looks like it's going to snow."

Talon and T-Bear scamper into the sled as Mushom releases the foot brake. "Aiee!" he yells. Freedom barks and starts off with the rest of the dog team following behind. Soon the sled is back up to speed. As they travel the remaining distance to Mushom's cabin, they keep silent, but their eyes reveal hope – hope that wasn't there before.

Maybe we'll be okay after all, Talon thinks to himself.

CHAPTER SIX
T-Bear's Plan

Flames crackle and hiss as they reach skyward from the split logs burning in the firepit between Mushom's cabin and the shore. Alphonse and Uncle Peter split more wood several metres away and Jacob carries the pieces over to a pile near the fire. Sarah and Raven sit around the blaze with Kohkum Rosalie, who checks on a large pot of tea hanging off a tripod made of green wood, directly over the fire.

"Almost ready," Kohkum Rosalie says as she puts the lid back on the pot.

"I can't wait for some of Aunt Anne's bannock," Raven says.

Kohkum Rosalie chuckles. "After eating your mushom's bannock, I would guess so." Sarah laughs at the remark but Raven takes offence.

"Mushom's bannock was fine," Raven says. "It was just a little chewy sometimes, and a little hard sometimes." Kohkum Rosalie and Sarah laugh again. Raven decides to be quiet, but she gives them another indignant look as Jacob deposits his load of firewood and turns to fetch some more where Uncle Peter and Alphonse continue to chop.

"You're right, my girl," Kohkum Rosalie says to appease her granddaughter, "your mushom's bannock isn't bad."

"Just not as good as Aunt Anne's," Sarah adds. Kohkum Rosalie bites her tongue. Raven shrugs at her mother and grandmother.

"No one's bannock is as good as Aunt Anne's," she tells them.

The cabin door suddenly opens and Aunt Anne steps out with two loaves of fresh bannock. Still hot from the oven, they emit steady billows of steam into the cold late afternoon air. "Yay!" Raven yells.

Uncle Peter and Alphonse stop their chopping and put down their axes as Jacob also stops and turns, heading straight for the bannock. Uncle Peter and Alphonse hurry after him, until they all catch themselves and try to play it cool, smiling at each other. Kohkum Rosalie makes room on the picnic table near the fire, where tin mugs wait to be filled with tea. Aunt Anne puts the bannock, half-wrapped in tea towels, onto the table along with a container of margarine and a butter knife.

"Make sure to save some for Cyril and the boys now," she tells everybody. Uncle Peter, Alphonse, and Jacob wait patiently as Raven tears off a small chunk of bannock from one of the loaves and lathers it with margarine. She bites into the morsel and savours the taste.

"Mmmmmm."

Kohkum Rosalie smiles at Raven. The men continue to wait as the women tear off their own pieces of bannock. Finally it's the men's turn. They share smiles as they tear off larger chunks than the others, but they're all careful not to take the largest piece, so they each wind up with pieces that are roughly the same size. Everyone eats in silence, savouring the hot bannock.

Uncle Peter is the first to notice something as he looks out over the frozen lake. Aunt Anne sees her husband's reaction and she looks out at the lake as well. One by one, the others notice Uncle Peter and Aunt Anne watching the frozen lake, and they all turn to look.

"Is that them?" Kohkum Rosalie asks, squinting hard. Uncle Peter nods.

Gradually the dogsled comes into view, Freedom charging forward and Mushom urging the whole team on. Shadow is right behind Freedom, running fluidly and with an easy rhythm, matching Freedom stride for stride. Freedom glances over his shoulder at Shadow, then turns back and charges hard to the shore.

"Aiee!" Mushom yells.

Kohkum Rosalie clucks her tongue and Aunt Anne nods. "That husband of yours has to slow down," says the best bannock maker in this part of northern Saskatchewan, though some would say she's the best anywhere. Her sister nods in agreement.

"If I've told him once..." Kohkum Rosalie starts.

Aunt Anne nods as Alphonse looks to Uncle Peter to see if he has an opinion. So does Jacob. "He's got a few years left in him yet," Uncle Peter states. "And if he has any food for us, you'll both have to eat your words." Aunt Anne and Kohkum Rosalie scowl playfully at Uncle Peter.

As the dog team gets closer, they all see Talon and T-Bear in the sled, looking back at them. "There are the boys," Sarah says, a big smile erupting on her face. Jacob nods. Sarah and the men get up to meet Mushom and his two grandsons, who ride the sled off the ice and up the shore on the well-worn trail. Mushom doesn't need to yell a command as Freedom knows what to do from years of repetition. He leads the team up to the front of the cabin, well away from the fire, and comes to a stop.

He pants heavily as Shadow and the other dogs stop behind him. All the dogs pant to catch their breath and replenish their bodies with oxygen, though Shadow appears far less winded from the run than Freedom is. In much the same way, Talon and T-Bear look fresh compared to Mushom's weariness. Kohkum Rosalie and

Aunt Anne observe Mushom, then both turn and look at Uncle Peter. Uncle Peter doesn't look back.

"Anything?" Uncle Peter asks his brother. Mushom shakes his head. The entire camp seems to sigh all at once, save for Mushom, Talon, and T-Bear. Talon and T-Bear hop out of the sled as Mushom applies the foot brake.

"I see you were able to put up the tent," Mushom says, motioning to the trapline abode.

"We're not useless," Jacob responds, half in jest, as T-Bear and Talon race over to their respective parents. Jacob opens his arms for T-Bear as Talon hugs Alphonse and Sarah.

"You helping your mushom good?" Sarah asks Talon.

Talon nods. "We pulled out the nets and checked the traps," he tells his parents as the others listen.

"And we nearly got a deer," T-Bear chimes in to Jacob. "But it got away."

"Really," Kohkum Rosalie says as she rises and walks over to her husband.

"It's true," Mushom admits to her. "And yes, it was because of my eyes, and yes, I know you want me to slow down." Kohkum smiles as she reaches him. "And yes, the boys were a big help," Mushom finishes.

"The animals are telling you to slow down, Cyril," Aunt Anne tells Mushom. Mushom gives her a sour look.

"You still have tomorrow," Kohkum Rosalie tells him and gives him a big hug.

"We still have tomorrow," Uncle Peter repeats.

Kohkum releases Mushom from her grip and takes his cheeks in her hands. "I missed you, you old fart," she tells him with a toothless smile. The other members of the extended family all chuckle as Mushom smiles at his wife. He has more of his original teeth in place.

"I missed you too," he replies. They share a kiss as Talon and T-Bear have their hair tousled by their parents.

Aunt Anne and Uncle Peter smile at the displays of affection before she motions to the picnic table. "I made some fresh bannock," she announces.

Mushom, T-Bear, and Talon turn away from their respective loved ones and make beelines to the picnic table and Aunt Anne's bannock. Kohkum Rosalie smiles and shakes her head as everyone else has another good chuckle. "Tea should be ready," she tells them.

They all gather around the fire, each taking a tin mug as Kohkum Rosalie lifts the teapot off the fire with an oven mitt to protect her hands. She takes it around, filling their mugs, and the family sits and drinks their tea and eats their bannock as the sun begins to set, spreading a pink and purple hue over the vast, snow-covered land.

T-Bear stops to flex his right hand, a blister having formed in the palm. Jacob sees it and motions towards it. "It's a lot of work out here, isn't it?" he asks his son.

T-Bear nods and Jacob smiles. "Are you ready to go home yet?"

T-Bear looks at his father. "I was kind of hoping I could stay here longer. It's fun, Dad," T-Bear tells him. Jacob nods, as his smile slips a bit.

Mushom looks at Jacob as he chews his bannock. "How was the trip?" Jacob shrugs that it was fine and Mushom nods. "I'm glad everyone made it safely."

They all finish their bannock and sip their tea quietly over the next few minutes. Mushom wipes his mouth and nods at Uncle Peter. "How much food is there?"

Uncle Peter finishes chewing the last of his bannock and he swallows as he wipes his hands. "Not enough for everyone arriving today. If this is all we have for Christmas, we'll have to go back to our traplines tomorrow."

Raven stands up in front of the fire. "No!" she yells. "Everyone just got here."

"We will see what it is like tomorrow, my girl," Mushom tells her. Raven nods and walks over to Mushom.

"Tomorrow we'll get something," Raven says and kisses Mushom on the cheek. As Mushom smiles, Raven runs off, down the hill to the shore. "I'm going sliding," she yells over her shoulder.

Talon gets up. "I better go too," he says, pretending it's a major sacrifice as he saunters after her. T-Bear watches them, contemplating. Aunt Anne watches him, then reaches over and ruffles his hair.

"You're getting to be a big bear now," Aunt Anne tells him.

T-Bear soaks up the praise. "I'm going to be the biggest and greatest hunter in the north," he tells them. "I know how to hunt and trap and fish and everything."

Mushom smiles at T-Bear. "You can't hunt if there is nothing left," Mushom teaches his grandson. "Take only what you need, my boy, and nothing more. That is our agreement with the Creator."

T-Bear nods as Jacob kneels down to look his son in the face. "Did you listen to your mushom?" Jacob asks T-Bear.

"Of course I did. We learned how to do all kinds of stuff, like setting traps, bait, making snowshoes. You know...hunter stuff."

"Hunter stuff, eh?" Jacob says with a smile. T-Bear nods. "Well, you still have to pay attention to your schooling, you know."

Uncle Peter clucks his tongue as he gets up and walks away. T-Bear follows him. Jacob watches before he turns to the others.

"I'm just saying he needs to learn math and writing more than this hunter stuff," Jacob says.

"Don't start that again, Jacob," Mushom tells him. "He's still just a boy."

"Yeah," Jacob replies, "but you need certain skills to..." He voice trails off as he sees everyone looking at him crossly. "I mean things change and..." He trails off again and gives up.

The sun touches the horizon, casting striped shadows from the trees throughout the camp. For a moment the adults watch T-Bear join his two cousins as they play at the sliding area. Mushom lowers his head and closes his eyes.

"I am thankful to the grandfathers and grand-mothers for allowing everyone a safe journey here," he says in prayer. "I am pleased to see the grandchildren playing where I used to play as a young boy." He pauses to look around.

"As you all know, the fire has changed the animals and the land. We do not have enough food to make this Christmas visit as long as other years. We have some fish, and though it's not enough for everyone, no one will leave here empty-handed. We do not know if the animals will recover this year, so we'll have to reduce our gathering on our traplines, as the old ones did in times of need. It will affect all of us. *Ekosi.*"

An agreeable murmur follows around the fire.

"It's getting late," Mushom says, "and colder. That storm will be here tomorrow, so we'd better prepare." Mushom slowly gets up and stretches his back as the others walk to the cabin to begin preparations.

T-Bear, Talon, and Raven sit at the top of the small hill by the shore and look at the sunset. "If I had been hunting, I would have had two moose by now," T-Bear announces. "Mushom taught me how to track and hunt."

Raven looks at T-Bear and laughs. "You would not get two mooses," she tells T-Bear.

"Mushom taught me too," Talon tells his older cousin.

Raven slides down the small hill and onto the shore. T-Bear turns to Talon and speaks quietly. "You and I should go then," he says.

"Go where?" Talon asks with a quizzical look.

"Hunting and trapping," T-Bear responds. "You and me, we'll show them that we can hunt and trap and everyone won't have to leave on Christmas Eve."

"I don't think that's a good idea, T-Bear," Talon says gravely, shaking his head

"I thought you said you knew how to hunt?" T-Bear challenges. Talon remains silent. "All we have to do is follow the trails that Mushom showed us," T-Bear continues. "You remember where he put that marker for those moose tracks?" Talon remains quiet. "I'll be the guide if you forget," T-Bear adds.

"I remember," Talon says, annoyed.

"Good," T-Bear answers. "We'll leave early in the morning when everyone's asleep."

Raven trudges back up the hill and looks at the boys suspiciously. "What are you guys talking about?"

"Nothing, Raven," T-Bear says.

"Yeah," Talon adds, backing T-Bear up, "just hunter stuff."

Raven remains suspicious. "Hunter stuff, huh? You two couldn't trap a mouse." T-Bear and Talon look at each other and laugh.

"Let's get back to the cabin," Talon says, "it's getting cold." They all start back towards camp.

"Raven," T-Bear says, catching his younger cousin's attention. "You don't call them mooses. You say 'two moose.'"

Raven looks at Talon for confirmation. Talon nods. "It's like if I have a goose, what would three of them be?"

"You would have three gooses," she replies.

Talon and T-Bear share another laugh as they reach the two dog teams in front of the cabin. The dogs wag their tails as the kids pass. Talon pats Freedom as Raven pets Shadow. As the children reach the front door and step inside, Freedom and Shadow glare at each other.

CHAPTER SEVEN
Raven's Surprise

The winter moon is hardly more than a sliver in the night sky, but it shines and reflects off the snow, giving Mushom and Jacob enough light to finish tying a windbreak tarp to the trees beside the white trapline tent. The tent is aglow from the light within, smoke rising from the metal chimney poking through the tent roof above the wood stove inside. Jacob holds the lines in place as Mushom fastens the knot and pulls it tight. Done, they let go and watch the tarp ease into position, buffeted slightly by a strong breeze. The tarp settles and holds, and Mushom nods.

"That should do it."

Jacob bundles himself up and starts for the tent. Mushom stays where he is.

"We need water for the morning," Mushom tells him. Jacob stops, turns and stares at his father for a moment, then smiles and shakes his head.

"Aw! You always pick on me," Jacob tells his father in a teasing voice. Mushom laughs and steps over to the cabin, where he grabs two pails. Jacob follows and Mushom hands him the pails.

"Here," Mushom says. Jacob takes them and Mushom grabs a hatchet and one more pail for himself before he starts towards the shore, a large smile spreading across his face. Jacob smiles too and he follows. Mushom looks over his shoulder at his son and they break into laughter as Jacob catches up.

"I always pick on you because I know you're able to finish what you start," Mushom tells his son. Jacob takes it as a compliment before he turns and sees his father's face turn serious. Something is on Mushom's mind, and Jacob knows it. He waits for the old man to speak, and Mushom does.

"I know you are used to the city, but this is how you were raised. This is where your spirit is." He pauses for a moment as they walk on. "I can see it in T-Bear," he continues. "He needs your encouragement and support."

Jacob thinks about this for a moment as they navigate down the hill. "I could have used a bit of that when I left for the city," he replies.

Mushom nods. "I know now to let go and let you live your life the way you want to."

"I want T-Bear to have a good education."

"He will, but he likes to be out here. He enjoys it. You need to have faith in the boy. I know your heart was never in it, but I can see it in his spirit."

They walk quietly until they come to the water hole on the lake. Mushom sets his pail down on the ice and takes a long look around, the love for this land revealed in his eyes. "I always hoped to leave this trapline for you someday," he finally says.

Jacob looks around as well, but his eyes care less than Mushom's. "If he came out here once a year..."

"That's not enough," Mushom replies.

"I can't take him out of school."

Mushom pulls out the hatchet before he looks directly at his son. "You don't want this trapline, I know that. But T-Bear might, and if he does, he needs to learn." He stops there for a moment, staring at his son, imploring him. "I don't know how much longer I can wait," he adds.

Mushom continues to look at Jacob, who nods and lets out a breath. Mushom turns and drops to one knee before he chops through the surface ice covering the water hole. Jacob stands behind him and looks up at the northern lights dancing over the lake.

Long after the two men have returned with their water, long after the camp goes dark and quiet, the northern lights continue their fancy dance in the sky, green wisps melding with red and pink before they flee the dawn's early eastern glow. Freedom stirs, but the other dogs remain asleep outside the cabin and the trapline tent.

Inside the tent, with his boots already on, T-Bear quietly sneaks over to Talon, who lies fast asleep beside his sister and their parents. T-Bear reaches him and taps him on the shoulder. Talon opens his bleary eyes and sees T-Bear hovering over him, his finger to his lips telling Talon to be quiet.

"Let's go," T-Bear whispers at him.

"You're crazy!" Talon whispers back. "Let's wait to go with Mushom to check the traps." T-Bear looks around at the others and motions for Talon to be quiet again, then T-Bear grabs his coat, mitts, and toque and starts crawling towards the tent's door. When he gets there, he turns to the two duffel bags on the floor and picks one of them up. Talon watches him for a moment before he grabs his own boots and starts to put them on.

Moments later, T-Bear and Talon quietly slip out of the old tent into the light blue morning, each holding one of the duffel bags. Freedom and Shadow wake up and stir and Talon throws some fish scraps on the ground beside them to keep them quiet. Freedom and Shadow snatch up chunks of the fish as the other dogs come to life and do the same. Talon watches the dogs for a moment as he and T-Bear put their duffel bags in the sled and study the contents.

"The tent is here, some blankets, dishes, and stuff for cooking. Pretty much everything we need," Talon whispers. One of the blankets is made of bearskin. Talon turns and picks up a pair of medium-sized traps from beside the cabin as T-Bear turns and walks around towards the back.

"Where you going?" Talon asks in a whisper.

"Just wait," T-Bear tells his cousin. "I have to get something else." T-Bear runs behind the cabin as Talon puts the traps in the sled and waits. Several seconds later, T-Bear returns, a rifle in his hands. He holds it up to show Talon.

"Just in case we see that moose," T-Bear whispers.

Talon does not think this is a good idea and it shows in the look on his face.

"We are not going to have enough food from just trapping," T-Bear whispers at him. "We need to think big." T-Bear places the rifle in the sled as they both hear the tent flap opening. The boys turn, and to their surprise, Raven crawls out, fully dressed and with her own duffel bag.

"Are we going now?" Raven whispers.

"What do you mean, 'we'?" T-Bear whispers back. "Why should we take you?"

Raven looks at her brother. He shakes his head. "It's too dangerous," Talon whispers. "Go back to sleep."

"I'm going with you guys," Raven whispers in return. "You two argue too much and you need a referee."

"We don't need a referee," T-Bear replies.

Raven shrugs. "Let's see what Mushom thinks." With that, she turns and starts for the cabin door. T-Bear and Talon see where she's going and share looks of concern.

"Okay," Talon whispers at her.

Raven stops and turns. "Really?" she asks.

"Yeah," T-Bear mutters softly. "Just be quiet."

Raven giggles as she walks over and gets in the sled. "Besides, I brought food. Bet you guys didn't," she says.

Talon and T-Bear share a look and it's clear neither one of them thought of it. Raven climbs in with her duffel bag, carefully avoiding the rifle. Talon steps over to Freedom and takes the dog by the line attached to his harness. Freedom stands and leads the rest of the team to the front of the sled. T-Bear helps Talon tie them in place. When they finish, both boys start for the back of the sled before they realize where they're both going.

"I've had more practice than you," Talon says.

Reluctantly, T-Bear nods and he climbs inside the sled behind Raven. Talon continues around to the back and puts his left foot on the left runner. With his right foot he releases the foot brake and grabs the lines, pulling them gently to eliminate the slack. The wind suddenly increases, shaking the tarp protecting the tent. A coyote's call in the distance grabs their attention next, and they all look at each other and instinctively fasten their coats up to their necks, Talon holding the dog team lines under his arm. Done, he takes the lines in his hands and gives them a slight tug.

"Aiee," he whispers at the dog team.

Sensing the need for quiet, Freedom eases forward, with Shadow and the other dogs on his heels. The sled creaks over the hard-packed snow as it slowly moves away from the cabin, Freedom turning for the start of the trail, Talon hanging on to the lines tightly. Down the small hill, Freedom breaks into a slight run, the team obediently following as the children hang on. The nose of the sled teeters over the decline before the whole thing tips forward and down, gaining speed as the dogs keep running to stay ahead. When the sled levels out and slows down on the shore, the dogs pull the lines taut and jerk it back up to speed. Talon, T-Bear, and Raven all pitch backwards, but manage to hold on. On the frozen lake and its smooth trail, T-Bear and Raven relax in the sled and begin to enjoy the ride.

At the back, Talon's hands remain tightly clutched around the lines, his facial expression intense, complete with frown ripples between his eyebrows. Already second-guessing himself, he can imagine the disappointment on his mushom's face when they get back to camp, not to mention the angry look sure to be on his parents' faces. He sighs, knowing they're all going to be in trouble, but less so if they manage to bring home enough food for Christmas.

As concerns and worries continue to flash through Talon's thoughts, the sled glides gracefully across the frozen northern expanse, towards the sun as it peers over the eastern horizon. To the west, unseen by all three children, dark grey storm clouds form a ribbon above the horizon as the wind picks up again.

CHAPTER EIGHT
Green Bait and Pemmican Sandwiches

Freedom strides across another part of the frozen lake system that runs through Mushom and Uncle Peter's traplines. Shadow and the other dogs keep pace, as T-Bear and Raven remain comfortably in the sled. At the back, Talon hangs on a little harder than he needs to. He steers the team towards land and the dogs race to shore, hauling the sled up a trail that cuts through the rugged shoreline to a piece of level ground where the bush comes close to the water.

"Whoa!" Talon yells. The dogs come to a halt and the sled does as well. As Talon uses all his strength and weight to apply the foot brake, T-Bear and Raven climb out and stretch.

"Let's set a snare here," T-Bear says.

Talon finally gets the foot brake deep enough into the snow and lets out a heavy sigh as he wearily sits against the sled. "Just a second," he says, catching his breath. "That's harder than it looks."

T-Bear grabs his duffel bag and pulls some snare wire out. Raven bangs her mitts together for warmth. They both wait for Talon. "Ready?" T-Bear finally asks. Talon nods and gets to his feet.

"We'll set one of the traps here," Talon says, pointing to the trail in the snow leading into the bushes. "Those are marten tracks, not rabbit." T-Bear studies the tracks for a moment as Talon pulls one of the medium-sized traps from the sled. T-Bear puts the snare wire back in his duffel bag and they all walk towards the bush. Talon leads them to a spot beside a clump of three small trees.

"Here?" T-Bear asks. Talon nods and puts the trap down, and all three of them clear out an area at the base of the trees. When they're done, Talon turns to T-Bear and motions to the trap.

"You know how to do it?"

T-Bear hesitates. "You go ahead," he says.

Talon grabs the trap and positions himself to set it. He pries it apart and sets the pin, then turns back to T-Bear. "Where's the bait?"

A frown comes to T-Bear's face. "I thought you brought some," he says.

"You were supposed to bring it," Talon tells his cousin with some annoyance.

"I got the rifle," T-Bear defends himself with a yell. "You could have brought it."

"I got the traps and I guided us here," Talon yells back.

The boys go quiet for a moment, both knowing the bait was something they both overlooked. T-Bear is mad at himself as much as his cousin. Talon wonders what else they may have overlooked.

"We can use the food I brought," Raven finally pipes up.

"That's for us to eat later, Raven," Talon says in a more calm-sounding voice. "We need a scent for the trap."

They all look at each other in silence before Talon finally kneels down at the trap. With his back to T-Bear and Raven, he picks his nose and pulls out a substantial piece of nasal mucous. He rubs the green goop over a part of the tree that hangs over the trap, then covers the mechanism with snow to conceal it before he gets up and faces his sister and his cousin.

"That'll have to do until we get something better," he tells them before he starts for the sled. T-Bear and Raven follow.

"What's going to have to do for now?" T-Bear asks.

"Yeah," Raven says, "what did you use?"

"Nothing," Talon says. "Let's just go. We still have a lot to do." With the wind gaining strength, Talon picks up the pace and T-Bear and Raven hustle after him. The sun is now entirely above the horizon as the dark grey clouds continue their approach from the west. The kids don't see the clouds as they hop back on the sled. Talon releases the foot brake.

"Aiee!" he shouts and leads the dog team east.

BACK AT MUSHOM'S CAMP, however, they do notice the dark grey clouds — they being all of them — Mushom, Kohkum Rosalie, Uncle Peter, Aunt Anne, Alphonse, Sarah, and Jacob standing outside, staring at the ominous storm clouds. Jacob turns and stares off in the other direction — the direction the kids went earlier.

"How far could they have gotten?" he asks.

"Depends when they got up," Mushom answers, chastising himself for sleeping a little too late this morning. Usually up before the first rays of light, Mushom knows he was tired and not feeling well, but if there was one morning to wake up on time, or even early, it would have been today. He shakes his head, also realizing he had perhaps given T-Bear and Talon too much praise for their work on the land. They obviously felt they were ready to go out alone, and as their teacher, he must have been the one to make them feel that way.

"They followed the trail I took them on yesterday," he says.

"Take my dog team," Uncle Peter tells him. "Alphonse and Jacob and I can walk out to my traps and check as many as we can before the storm arrives."

Alphonse gives Uncle Peter a look as Jacob turns to Mushom. "I'd rather go with you," Jacob tells him. It's on the tip of Mushom's tongue to tell Jacob that he would only slow him down, but he manages to hold it back.

"Your father will travel faster if he goes alone," Uncle Peter advises Jacob. Jacob reluctantly nods, knowing his uncle speaks the truth, and knowing there's no one who knows the land in this area better than his father.

Without another word, Mushom walks over to Uncle Peter's dog team and releases the foot brake. "Aiee!" he yells, and the dogs spring to life, all of them barking as they move down the hill towards the lake with Mushom urging them on. "Aiee!" he yells again as they leave shore and accelerate onto the frozen lake.

The rest of the family remains on shore, watching, concern etched in all their faces. Kohkum Rosalie looks at them all and sees their worry. "That old man will find them," she announces. "He knows where to look."

Uncle Peter and Aunt Anne nod. Alphonse, Sarah, and Jacob just hope the old people are right. "Nothing we can do now but get ready," Aunt Anne tells Sarah with a sympathetic look. Sarah nods as Jacob turns to his aunt.

"Get ready for what?" he asks.

"To either stay and have a big family Christmas or split up and go to our separate traplines," she tells him.

"We'll have to do one or the other by the end of the day." Jacob nods. So do the other men.

Aunt Anne looks at the three of them and raises her eyebrows. "It would be nice if you found enough in the traps for everyone to stay," she tells them. The men nod again. "So you can leave anytime," she adds sarcastically.

Uncle Peter, Alphonse, and Jacob all give Aunt Anne surprised looks and she stares right back at them, nodding towards her husband's trapline to accentuate her point.

Uncle Peter bundles up. "Guess we should get going," he tells the two younger men, as though it was his idea. Alphonse and Jacob bundle up too, as Uncle Peter grabs his rifle and turns for the back of the cabin. Alphonse grabs a hatchet and follows. Empty-handed, Jacob follows as well.

The women watch for a moment, then they all share a smile and start for the cabin, though Sarah stops to look at her father leading her uncle's dog team out over the lake, the worried expression creeping back over her face. Kohkum Rosalie and Aunt Anne stop with her. They give her a few moments before Kohkum Rosalie takes her gently by the arm.

"C'mon," she says. "Your father will find them."

"I trust those boys on the land more than I trust Jacob out there," Aunt Anne adds. Sarah nods as she allows herself to be led to the cabin.

TALON DRIVES THE DOG TEAM to the shore of another island. "Whoa!" he yells, pulling the dogs to another stop. "This is where we'll set the snare," Talon tells his cousin as he sets the foot brake. As Talon walks to the front of the sled, T-Bear again digs in his duffel bag for his snare wire and Raven digs in her own duffel bag.

"I'll make a lunch," Raven announces as she pulls out a bundle and unwraps it to reveal bannock, pemmican, and lard. Talon pulls some fish scraps from the front of the sled and tosses them over for the dogs, who each snatch their fair share. T-Bear walks over to the rabbit trail and Talon hustles to catch up. When they reach the trail, T-Bear holds out the snare wire and he and Talon get to work, though they have trouble coordinating their actions.

"Hold it like this more," T-Bear says, tugging and twisting at the wire to try and show Talon what he means.

"No, it has to be more like this," Talon retorts, pulling and twisting at the wire as well.

"Give it here," T-Bear says, trying to yank it out of Talon's hands. Talon hangs on tight and yanks it back.

"*You* give it here," Talon answers. The boys continue their tug of war as Raven watches, spreading the pemmican and lard on pieces of bannock.

"If there are any rabbits around here, they're laughing at both of you," she yells at them. T-Bear and Talon stop and look at Raven, then look at each other, and both break into laughter. "Real funny," she says as she bites into her bannock and pemmican sandwich. The boys turn and see the food in her hand.

"Let's eat," T-Bear says, and he lets Talon have the snare wire as they walk over to the sled for their bannock and pemmican sandwiches. They sit with their food and all eat in silence as the wind whips at them in gusts.

"Maybe we should have left a note for them," Talon says after swallowing a mouthful. T-Bear chews a mouthful as he puts his sandwich down and reaches into the sled and grabs the rifle. He pulls it out and aims it across the bay as Talon moves Raven safely behind himself.

"We will be back with a lot of food and they'll all be surprised," T-Bear says, his left eye closed and his right lining up some target out over the lake. He pretends to pull the trigger. "Boom!" he yells.

Raven wraps her arms tight around her body and shivers. "How much longer are we going to be gone?" she asks. "It's getting cold, you guys."

Talon shrugs. "If the weather holds, we may be out here for awhile," he tells her.

"We still have to track that moose," T-Bear adds.

Raven stands and stares at the boys, her arms crossed, pouting, then her eyes fix on something behind them and she points. "What about that?"

The boys turn and suddenly see the dark clouds coming towards them in a large bank that runs the entire width of the sky. "We've gotta go T-Bear," Talon says as he quickly gets to his feet.

T-Bear remains where he is, the dark clouds holding his attention. "What is it?" he asks.

"It's a snowstorm," Talon says as he wolfs down the rest of his food. "We have to go."

T-Bear shakes his head. "We can't go back to Mushom's cabin. That's the direction it's coming from."

Talon pauses on his way back to the sled to study the clouds and gauge the wind. "You're right," he says, putting the snare wire back in T-Bear's duffel bag. He looks around and points to the far mainland. "Let's head towards that shore, we have to get off the lake."

"If we go that way," T-Bear says, as he points in a line parallel to the approaching clouds, "we may be able to get around it."

Talon shakes his head. "We won't be able to move fast enough. It's too big."

The severity of the situation finally hits Raven. "It's gonna hit us wherever we go," she says, her eyes big with concern.

"Yeah," Talon says before he points at the far mainland again. "But over there, we can at least find some shelter where we can put up a tent."

They all think about it for a moment, glancing around, trying to take stock of their situation, and slowly T-Bear and Raven also realize the inevitable – they're going to get caught in the storm and have to ride it out in the tent.

T-Bear finally nods. "Sounds good," he says.

Raven nods too. "Yeah."

T-Bear and Raven jump in the sled as Talon hustles to the back and releases the foot brake. Once on the runners, he grabs the handlebars and hangs on tight. "Aiee!" he yells. "Go, Freedom!"

Hearing the urgency in Talon's voice, Freedom barks and starts off hard with Shadow and the other dogs barking wildly as they follow suit. Soon the sled glides quickly over this part of the frozen lake, as the dogs reach their full speed, and T-Bear and Raven steal repeated glances at the fast-approaching storm.

Talon keeps his eyes on the far mainland, willing it to come closer. We'll make it, he tells himself. We have to make it.

CHAPTER NINE
The Storm

The snow starts to fall and the wind intensifies, as the dogs take the children closer to another of the vast lake's many shorelines. T-Bear and Raven remain huddled in the sled as Talon guides the dogs. Then something to his left catches his eye. As Talon turns to get a better look, T-Bear and Raven catch sight of it too – a towering, swirling mass of snow spinning towards them.

"Whoa!" Talon cries out, and Freedom leads the rest of the team to a quick stop, the sled stopping with them as Talon leans on the brake. The children stand and watch the swirling mass pass them and move on down the lake as the storm continues to build. Then, as quickly as it came, the twisting column of snow dissipates and vanishes.

"What was that?" Raven asks, yelling above the noise of the storm.

"I think it was a snow devil," Talon replies. "Mushom told me about them once." He braces himself on the back of the sled and T-Bear and Raven take it as a cue to get ready as well. "Aiee!" Talon yells and Freedom leads the dog team back into a run, tugging the sled along and slowly building speed.

Raven looks over her shoulder and gasps, then points repeatedly. "Here comes another one," she yells. The boys look over their shoulders as well and see another large, swirling mass of snow coming towards them. "Faster, Talon!" Raven shouts.

"I'm trying!" Talon shouts back. "Aiee!"

The dogs increase their speed, but they're no match for the spinning snow devil as it quickly catches up and engulfs them. The kids try to shield themselves from the stinging winds as best they can while the dogs turn away, slowing their pace and taking them off course.

"I can't see a thing," T-Bear shouts.

"Just hang on," Talon yells at him. "It'll pass soon."

And it does, almost vanishing while it's on top of them. Raven breathes a sigh of relief as the dog team corrects its course and charges for the shoreline, the storm slowly gaining strength around them. "Aiee!" Talon shouts again, urging them on.

The dog team charges on. Freedom leads and barks to keep the rest of the team in proper stride. Most of the dogs are beginning to labour, but Freedom and Shadow maintain the pace, almost pulling the others with them as the shoreline draws near. As they approach, Talon searches for a trail up to the shelter of the trees and rocks, but the shoreline is rugged and the new snow covers any trails. Freedom leads the dog team off the lake and onto the shore, and they stop in front of a steep hill. The children all look up at the formidable obstacle, Talon still trying to figure out a way up.

"It's too steep," Raven yells. "We'll never make it."

"There's a trail between those rocks – look," Talon tells them, pointing up the hill.

"I think Raven's right," T-Bear says.

"We can't go back," Talon responds. "We have to find shelter. Aiee, Freedom!"

Freedom barks and leads the dog team up the steep embankment, as the children hang on tight. Initially the climb isn't so severe, but as they get further up the hill, the team's pace becomes laboured as they struggle to keep forward momentum.

"Aiee!" Talon shouts again as Freedom and Shadow both bark at the other dogs, who all strain as the full weight of the sled grips them. The steepness of the hill, and the increased weight because of it, slows the dogs to a crawl and they pant from the exertion. The sled leans to one side as the dogs continue to pull.

"Lean the other way," Talon shouts and T-Bear and Raven listen as they try to even out the sled. The load finally becomes too much for the dogs and they come to a stop a few metres from their goal. With the top of the hill so tantalizingly close, Talon lets out an almost inaudible groan because he knows what's going to happen next.

"We're not gonna make it," Raven laments.

The dogs struggle to keep the sled in place, but gravity slowly does its work, and the sled, dog team, children and all begin to slide backwards. The dogs dig their claws into the snow in a vain effort to hold on, but the speed of their descent only increases when the sled's skis snag under some brush and they start to tip over.

"Hang on!" Talon yells and they all do as the sled tips and tips and finally rolls over, whipping the dogs down the hill where some of them hit the rocks hard, including Freedom. The children and all the supplies are dumped into the snow, and the sled rolls over again before it hits some rocks and comes to a stop.

For a moment only the storm can be heard before T-Bear manages to stand up. "Are you two okay?" he asks.

"I'm okay," Talon replies.

"Me too," says Raven. They all dust the snow off their clothes and survey the damage. "Now what are we going to do?" Raven asks. "I knew we shouldn't have left the cabin." Talon gives his sister an exasperated look.

"Well, how was I supposed to know we would hit a storm?" T-Bear says, knowing this was all his idea.

"Let's try and push it up the hill," Talon says before he whistles at the dogs. The dogs, except for one, climb back up until the lines are taut, as the children take positions on the bottom side of the sled.

"Push!" Talon yells. "Aiee!"

The children push and the dogs pull, but the sled barely budges and they give up after several seconds.

"It's no use," T-Bear says.

Raven spots Freedom lying down near the sled. "How come Freedom's not up front?" she asks.

Talon steps around the sled and sees Freedom lying there, whimpering. "Freedom wasn't pulling," he says, "no wonder we couldn't move it."

"What's the matter with him?" Raven asks with worry.

Talon climbs up to the dog and puts his hand on Freedom's right flank. Freedom yelps in pain and Talon quickly pulls his hand away. Freedom licks Talon's hand and weakly wags his tail.

"Freedom's hurt," Talon announces.

Raven and T-Bear scramble over to the hurt dog as Freedom manages another wag of his tail. "What's wrong with him?" T-Bear asks. Talon shakes his head to say he doesn't know. Raven starts to cry.

"Don't cry, Raven," Talon tells his sister in a comforting voice. "Everything will be okay." T-Bear gives Talon a "yeah, right" look, but Talon frowns at him to keep his mouth shut.

"Let's set up the tent," Talon instructs. T-Bear nods and slides back down the hill to dig for the tent among the dumped supplies as Raven holds Freedom's head in her lap. "We'll put a blanket underneath him and pull him up that way," Talon tells her. Raven nods, gently petting the top of Freedom's head. Talon slides down the hill to help his cousin, who holds up a bundle of canvas.

"This is it," T-Bear tells him.

Talon nods, looking at the contents of the sled slowly getting covered with snow. "We'll have to carry everything up the hill," he says.

"Freedom too?" T-Bear asks.

Talon nods again. "Freedom too."

T-Bear grabs a couple more items and starts the climb up the slope as Talon gathers a few more of the spilled supplies before following. Raven stays with Freedom, who lies still save for the tip of his tail, which wags, but really no more than a twitch.

The boys return and Talon looks over at his sister. "We're going to need some firewood, Raven," he says. Raven nods and gently slips Freedom's head off of her lap, balancing on the uneven slope. T-Bear slides down to gather more supplies, while Talon moves over to the dog team and Raven climbs the hill. Carefully, Talon unhitches Freedom's line from the others before he leads them up and out of the way. The dogs follow but seem confused, unsure. Shadow is at the back, looking down at Freedom, who watches from below.

"C'mon, Shadow," Talon says with some impatience. He pulls on the line, tugging at Shadow's harness, and the dog turns and obeys.

Talon climbs to the crest of the hill and the dogs follow until they come over the top. Several metres away, and down another slope, is their pile of supplies salvaged from below, in a flat area protected from the wind by large rocks and dense stands of bush. Talon leads the dogs to one of the stands of bush a few metres from the pile and ties them there. The dogs lie together, forming a large heap of fur in the ever-deepening snow. T-Bear comes over the top of the hill with another load of supplies and carries them down to the pile, gently dropping them before he puts his hands on his knees to catch his breath.

"Is that all of it?" Talon asks. T-Bear nods as Raven steps out of the bush with an armful of dry branches. She drops them in the snow a few metres from the supplies and looks at her brother and cousin as the snow begins to fall harder. Talon grabs a blanket from the pile and opens it up as he moves back to the hill.

"Let's get Freedom," Talon says. Raven and T-Bear follow him back down the hill, sliding to the injured dog. Talon puts the blanket against the ground directly behind and nearly underneath the dog. "It's his back right leg, I think," Talon tells them, "so try not to touch it."

Raven begins to pet Freedom again as Talon and T-Bear get on either side of the blanket and each grab a top corner. Carefully they slide the leading edge of the blanket underneath Freedom, who twitches and adjusts his weight slightly as they get further along.

"It's okay, boy," Raven says, still stroking the dog's head. "Everything will be all right."

Talon and T-Bear, now holding the bottom corners of the blanket as well, get it entirely underneath the dog and begin to support him so he won't slide down the hill. "Ready?" Talon asks. T-Bear nods and they lift Freedom off the hard ground of the steep slope with the blanket. Raven gets out of the way as the boys carefully make their way back up the hill. "Get behind us, Raven, and help if we start having trouble."

Raven scurries down the hill a bit before she stops and turns to follow them closely. The boys manage to reach the top without her help, but Raven remains at the ready until they get Freedom safely onto flat ground near their makeshift camp. Gently the boys lower the dog to the ground and let him continue to lie on the blanket. Raven goes to Freedom immediately and pets him again as the dog wags his tail a little more strongly. Talon and T-Bear watch as they catch their breath and stretch out their aching muscles.

"We need more firewood," Talon tells his sister.

Raven gives him an annoyed look. "What about you guys?" she asks.

"We have to set up the tent," T-Bear tells her. Raven gets to her feet in a huff and stomps back into the bush as Talon and T-Bear grab the canvas tent and open it up.

"How will they know where we are?" T-Bear asks. "You know, if they come looking for us? We've never come here with Mushom before and our trail will be covered with snow."

Once the tent is completely spread out, they grab the wooden poles and pegs from the supply pile as Talon mulls T-Bear's question over and over in his mind. "Mushom knows this land better than anyone else," he finally says. "And I may have come here with him once before."

"May have?" T-Bear asks.

"I'm not sure," Talon admits.

They continue to work on the tent as Raven returns with a second load of branches and drops them on her first pile. Without a word she goes back into the bush for more. The boys also work in silence and the tent slowly takes shape. The site is protected from the full force of the wind by the surrounding bush and landscape, but enough makes it through to catch the canvas and make the job difficult. As Raven drops her last load on the large pile, the boys tie off the last part of the tent, and it finally stands finished, the canvas shell rippling as the buffeting wind continues to increase in strength.

"We have shelter," T-Bear remarks.

"Now what?" Raven asks.

"Build a fire?" T-Bear suggests.

Talon nods and drops to the supplies to dig through one of the bags. Not finding what he's looking for, he searches another and another before he finally turns to T-Bear with some alarm. "Where are the matches?" he asks.

T-Bear immediately becomes concerned and so does Raven. "Where did you put them?" T-Bear asks accusingly.

"They're supposed to be in the one of the bags," Talon replies defensively. "And they're not."

"Why didn't you bring some?" T-Bear asks.

"Why didn't you?' Talon counters. "This was your idea."

"I can't think of everything," T-Bear says. "Look again."

Talon digs through the bags again as T-Bear and Raven watch. A thought hits Raven. "Maybe they fell out in the sled or something," she says.

Talon and T-Bear share a look before T-Bear turns and trots off. Talon turns back to the duffel bags and searches the last one for the second time.

T-Bear steps over the crest of the hill and slides down to the overturned sled. Snow is gathering in a thickening layer on its underside. T-Bear digs around both in the sled and in the surrounding snow, but he finds nothing and gives up.

Talon and Raven watch expectantly when T-Bear comes back over the hill and ambles towards them. "Nothing," he says, shaking his head. The three of them stand there for several moments as the storm rages around them.

"We have to get into the tent and huddle for warmth," Talon says. "We'll go home when the storm passes."

The three of them gather the blankets and move over to the tent. Talon holds open the flap and Raven and T-Bear step inside. Talon crouches at the door and tosses them the blanket under his arm before he ties the flap shut behind them, shielding them from the storm even more.

Inside, the children work quickly and quietly, spreading out the blankets and lying down together for warmth, covering themselves with the large bearskin blanket. Their teeth chattering, they lie there, listening to the shaking tent.

"I'm cold," Raven says.

"We'll warm up in a minute," Talon assures her.

Outside, as the snow continues to fall heavily, Freedom manages to snuggle in with the other dogs, joining their big, warm mass of fur, their collective body heat protecting them from the cold. Shadow sniffs at Freedom and licks at the older dog's sore leg. Freedom licks the top of Shadow's head before he falls into a deep rest.

AT THE CABIN, Kohkum Rosalie, Aunt Anne, and Sarah sit at the table. Kohkum Rosalie and Sarah darn socks as Aunt Anne kneads a batch of dough for two more loaves of bannock. "It's all in the kneading," Aunt Anne tells them.

Sarah and Kohkum Rosalie are quiet for a moment, then Kohkum Rosalie speaks. "You've been saying that for thirty-five years," she says in a droll voice.

"If I have, it's because it's true," Aunt Anne retorts.

Kohkum Rosalie leans over to Sarah and whispers loud enough for Aunt Anne to hear. "I quit making bannock thirty-five years ago so she could keep bragging," she says, motioning to her sister.

"You quit because you make worse bannock than your husband does," Aunt Anne comes back.

"Ah!" Kohkum Rosalie rasps. Sarah smiles at their playful bickering before she turns to look out the window with a mix of hope and worry. Kohkum Rosalie and Aunt Anne glance at her as they continue working.

"Storm's getting really bad," Sarah finally says. They hear the wind howling outside and Aunt Anne turns to the window with hope and concern as well.

Only Kohkum Rosalie remains focused on her task. "They know what to do," she says.

"But they're so young," Sarah responds.

"And he's so old," Aunt Anne adds.

"They know what to do," Kohkum Rosalie repeats. As far as she's concerned, the discussion is over. Aunt Anne and Sarah remain quiet, but they continue to stare out the window at the raging storm, the pitch of the wind's howl rising and falling from octave to octave.

And then there are footsteps. Kohkum Rosalie hears them first, then the other two. They wait as the footsteps get closer and the front door of the cabin opens. Wind and snow sweep in as the three men, Uncle Peter, Alphonse, and Jacob, quickly step inside. Alphonse closes the door behind them to shut out the storm and Jacob drops to his knees and takes off his toque, exhausted. All three of them are covered in snow from head to foot with icicles hanging from their eyebrows. They wipe off the snow as they catch their breath, though Uncle Peter and Alphonse aren't nearly as winded as Jacob is.

"They back yet?" Uncle Peter asks.

Aunt Anne shakes her head and the shoulders of all three men slump ever so slightly.

"Get anything?" Aunt Anne asks. Uncle Peter shakes his head and the women go back to work.

"Got caught in the storm, eh?" Kohkum Rosalie says.

Alphonse points at Jacob, but it's Uncle Peter who speaks, and he addresses Kohkum Rosalie. "Your son couldn't keep up," Uncle Peter tells her. "We got caught in the storm because we had to wait for him."

"We walked ten miles out on the trapline," Jacob gasps as Alphonse and Uncle Peter climb out of their outerwear. "You walk ten miles out on the trapline, you have to walk ten miles back. But because of the storm they said we had to run..." He takes a few deep breaths and shakes his head. "I'm sorry."

Uncle Peter sneers at Jacob. "City boy," he mutters.

Alphonse sees Sarah go to the window and stare out at the storm, that look of concern bringing creases back to her forehead. Alphonse hangs up his coat and walks over and stands behind her, wrapping his arms around her shoulders. Sarah gives him a wan smile and rubs his arm before turning back to the window. Jacob takes off his outerwear and joins them as well. Uncle Peter joins the older women at the table and the three of them watch the younger adults for a moment, then share grave looks with each other.

"Think it'll get any worse?" Jacob asks about the storm.

"I hope not," Uncle Peter replies.

The wind's howl intensifies into a high-pitched squeal. Jacob and Sarah flinch.

Out on another part of the lake, Uncle Peter's dog team presses on through the almost blinding snow, pulling the sled with Mushom on the back as they're buffeted by the wind. Mushom holds the steering bow harder than usual, using it for support as another pain rips through the right side of his body. As it did the other times, it passes, but he knows the pains and whatever is causing them are taking their toll on his body. He feels fatigued and in a daze. He shakes his head to try and stay alert as the storm rages around him.

He reads the land and finds comfort in its familiarity — the outline of trees or low-lying hills appearing where they're supposed to be through breaks in the snowfall. The storm is a strong one, but he's seen others like it, been through others like it — many times. He thinks back, starting when he was a child, to the first of many storms weathered on knowledge passed down through many generations. He shakes his head again, forcing himself to stay in the present.

"Aiee!" he shouts at the dogs, familiar enough, but not his own. The dogs bark in response as he shivers and rubs his forehead, sweat dripping from his brow.

CHAPTER TEN
Reunion

The children continue to huddle inside the tent for warmth, the bearskin blanket wrapped tightly around them, with Raven in the middle. The canvas tent ripples and shakes in the fierce wind. A small snowdrift forms at the entrance where snow has found its way through the canvas door.

The children all look worried, none more than T-Bear. "I'm sorry, you guys," he tells them. "I thought we would be okay."

"It's all right, T-Bear," Talon tells him.

They hear Shadow bark outside and the other dogs gradually join in as the children listen. "What's that noise?" Raven asks. Talon and T-Bear can only hear the dogs, the wind, and the rattling tent, but soon something begins to register — something they can't recognize over the other loud sounds.

"What if it's a bear?" Raven asks with alarm.

"They're sleeping," Talon tells her.

"Wolves?" T-Bear suggests.

"I'd take wolves over a wolverine," Talon responds.

They listen to the dogs barking wildly outside the tent, along with the other unrecognizable sound, and then there's silence. They hold their breath and each other tightly when they hear crunching close by. Suddenly the tent door rattles and the flaps open up and Mushom pushes his face through.

"*Tansi*," he says, giving them a quick once-over.

"Mushom!" the children respond in unison. The children and their grandfather stare at each other for a moment, the children surprised, their grandfather not. T-Bear's guilt emerges.

"Mushom, I...I just wanted to get the moose," T-Bear manages, full of remorse.

Talon and Raven look at him and then each other with solemn faces before they turn to Mushom as well. "It was kinda my idea too," Talon says.

"Me too," says Raven.

T-Bear glances at his cousins as Mushom studies them all for a moment with a knowing look. Mushom finally reaches into his pocket and pulls out a box of wooden matches and holds them out for T-Bear. T-Bear extricates himself from the blankets and reaches out to take them as Mushom slides through the front door to the ground where he lies down, exhausted.

"Go start the fire," he says. T-Bear gets up and does what he's told, scrambling out of the tent quickly. Talon and Raven look at each other, not sure what to do.

"I better go help him," Talon says, and he gets up and follows his cousin.

Raven watches him go before turning back to her grandfather. He lies there, his head resting on the ground as he stares at the ceiling, trying to catch his breath, holding his right side.

"Are...are you okay, Mushom?" Raven asks in a quivering voice. "Are we going to be okay?"

Mushom nods. "We will be okay, my girl. Mushom just needs to rest awhile. We will try to go after we warm up."

Raven studies her grandfather closely before she crawls over to him, dragging the blankets along with her, and she lays two of the smaller blankets on the ground beside him. "Get on the blankets, Mushom," she says gently.

Mushom manages to shimmy over and Raven covers him with the bearskin blanket and uses the last of the smaller blankets to make a pillow. Mushom raises his head and Raven slides the pillow in place. "Good?" she asks when she's done and Mushom has lowered his head.

Mushom nods and closes his eyes. Raven lies down beside him and continues to study her grandfather, his breathing, the colour of his skin, his facial expression. She sees the perspiration on his brow and wipes it away with her sleeve. Mushom doesn't react. As far as Raven can tell, he may already be asleep.

Outside, T-Bear nurtures a small fire and Talon watches. The heavy snowfall presents a challenge, but T-Bear's body shields the tiny blaze from most of the elements as its flames leap into the dry branches above to feed itself. As more of the small branches catch fire, T-Bear reaches and Talon hands him some larger pieces. Soon the blaze becomes large enough for the boys to have to step away from its heat. T-Bear turns and walks to Uncle Peter's sled and digs around inside. He pulls out a long canvas bundle and returns, placing it near the fire. He sits on one end and gestures to the other, offering it to Talon. Seeing that the bundle is long enough for two, Talon sits and they watch the flames, the wood piled by Raven within arm's reach of T-Bear.

"You shouldn't have tried to lead the dogs up this hill," T-Bear says after a long silence.

Talon slowly turns and looks at his cousin. "We shouldn't even be out here," he replies coolly.

They continue to watch the fire in silence. The tent flap opens and Raven steps outside. She hustles over to the fire and stands as close as she can without catching flame or getting burned, and warms herself up enthusiastically.

"Oh yeah," she murmurs, soaking in the heat. She continues to stand close but turns to the boys, a serious look sweeping over her face. "Mushom is too warm, you guys. He doesn't look good."

"He'll be okay," T-Bear says. "Nothing can hurt Mushom."

"That's not what Kohkum and Aunt Anne say," she tells them. Talon and T-Bear look at her with renewed concern. They glance over at the tent as a strong gust of wind rips through the camp.

"We have to get back before it gets late," Talon says.

Just then the tent flap opens and Mushom steps out. He walks slowly over to the fire and Talon gets up so Mushom can sit. Mushom does, the fire adding the illusion of colour to his face. He stares at the flames, silent, his eyes glazed over. The children fidget as the silence becomes uncomfortable, then they lower their heads and listen to the howling gusts of wind while they wait for Mushom to speak.

Mushom gives his head a shake and blinks his eyes before fixing them back on the fire. "In your journey on Mother Earth, you will be guided by your emotions," he tells the young ones, "but you must never forget the Creator's gift to you...your knowledge."

"I'm sorry, Mushom," T-Bear says, trying to keep the tears from forming in his eyes. "I should never have left the gathering. It was my fault, not theirs," he motions to his cousins, then turns back to his idol. "I'll never be a great hunter like you."

Mushom pats his grandson on the knee. "You have already shown the grandfathers what you want. They will listen to your heart and it is up to you to follow it.

No one else can do that for you," he says, then adds, "your courage is strong. You just have to balance it with good judgment."

Mushom takes some sage from his pocket with his large right hand and holds it out. "Here."

The children hold out their hands, palms up, and Mushom deposits small amounts of sage in each hand. The children cup one hand and shield it with the other to protect the medicinal herb from the wind. Once they each have their share, they close their hands and wait. When he finishes, Mushom looks to the sky.

"I thank you for all that you have given us. I thank you for the animals that sustain us in our times of hunger. I thank you for the trees and rocks that shelter us when we are homeless. I thank you for the fire that warms us when we are cold. I thank you for the water that sustains us when we are thirsty. I'd also like to thank you for my grandchildren, who have opened up their hearts to try to find us food in our time of need. May you look kindly on their efforts and continue to guide them in their life's journey. *Aho!*"

With his eyes closed, Mushom drops the remaining sage in his hand on the fire. The smoke lifts up towards the trees as the wind dies down. Mushom nods to the children and they place their sage on the fire. As the additional smoke rises, Mushom returns his gaze to the sky.

"The storm's died down," he says, "but it'll start up again, maybe harder. We better start back."

"What about that moose?" T-Bear asks.

Mushom gives him a forlorn look. "I wanted that moose too," he says, then shrugs. "Sometimes things are meant to be. I'm just happy you children are learning these ways." Mushom stands up, wavering slightly in the dying wind and looks over at the dogs. "What's wrong with Freedom?" he asks.

"He got hurt when the sled tipped over," Talon explains. Mushom nods, then winces and grabs at his right side, doubling over in pain. The children watch, afraid, but when it looks like he might collapse, T-Bear and Talon grab him.

"Are you okay, Mushom?" Raven asks.

Mushom nods as he regains his balance. He stands on his own while the boys gradually let go. "I will be," he says. "You boys grab those dogs. It's time to go home now." Mushom grabs a coil of rope he brought with him and begins to tie it around his waist as the children share concerned looks. He picks up the remaining rope and sits back down at the fire before turning to the boys. "Go on," he tells them. The boys nod and start for the two dog teams as Mushom warms himself at the fire. Raven watches him closely and he winks at her. She manages a smile.

THE SLED LIES TIPPED OVER in the deep snow, a front corner wedged in a crevice. T-Bear and Talon have a dog team each on either side of the sled, while Mushom stands above, connected to it by the rope tied around his waist. Raven stands up top with Freedom.

"Okay," Mushom yells at the boys. "When I say pull, just ease the dogs up the hill slowly." The boys nod and Mushom digs his heels in, planting his feet firmly on the sloped ground, the rope gripped tightly in his hands. "Okay!" he yells.

"Aiee," the boys say with raised voices. The dogs move up the hill on either side as Mushom pulls from above. The sled creaks as its front corner lifts from the crevice.

"Now!" Mushom yells, setting his weight at an angle more parallel to the hill. As T-Bear leads Shadow and the rest of Mushom's dogs around to the other side of the sled, Talon scrambles to the sled itself and unties the dog team lines from the front, then reties them to the middle of one of the runners. Once the lines are in place, he joins T-Bear and both dog teams. "Go!" Mushom yells as he bears the entire weight of the sled.

"Aiee," the boys say again and the dogs move forward, Shadow and Mushom's team after a slight hesitation. Gradually the sled begins to turn over. As the dogs continue to pull, and Mushom struggles to hold the sled in place, the boys hustle back around to the other side and push until it finally flips upright. It slides down a few feet, pulling Mushom and the dogs with it, but they get their footing and manage to hold it steady.

"Hurry," Mushom says.

T-Bear takes Mushom's dogs back around to the other side as Talon rushes in to tie the lines back to the sled's front, once more causing Mushom to bear the full weight of the sled. Raven watches him closely and Freedom whines as Mushom grunts from the exertion. With the lines back in place, Talon hustles over to Uncle Peter's dogs, urging them over until their line is tight. T-Bear does the same with Mushom's dogs on the other side. "Okay!" Talon yells when they're done.

Mushom relaxes with a sigh of relief. Raven and Freedom look less anxious, too, as the dogs adjust their footing as the weight of the sled falls to them. "Okay, now ease them down the hill," Mushom says. T-Bear and Talon move down, ahead of the dogs, then both turn to face the leads.

"C'mon, boy," Talon tells Bear.

T-Bear makes smooching noises to Shadow on the other side. Both dog teams get the point and start easing down the hill, the sled creeping down with them. Mushom keeps pace from above as Raven and Freedom continue to watch from the top. Talon and T-Bear move down the hill ahead of the dogs, who keep a steady pace after them. Mushom sweats as he ambles down the hill, still tied to the sled. A few seconds later, the sled reaches flat ground and the boys and the dogs stop. Mushom huffs down the last few feet of the slope and unties the rope from his waist, coiling it up when he's finished. The children and the dogs all watch.

"Now what?" T-Bear finally asks.

"Pack up the sled," Mushom tells him, "get Uncle Peter's dogs tied to his sled, and we'll go." Talon unties Uncle Peter's dogs from Mushom's sled and leads them over to Uncle Peter's as T-Bear scrambles back up the hill. When Talon finishes with the dogs, he hurries after T-Bear. Mushom waits at the bottom, catching his breath. When the boys both pass Raven at the top of the hill, she continues to watch her grandfather who, with his back to her, suddenly drops to one knee and bends over, holding his right side.

Raven's bottom lip quivers slightly as Freedom whines. The boys, gathering supplies from the pile they made earlier, don't notice. "Get up, Mushom," Raven says quietly to herself, "please get up." Freedom barks and Mushom suddenly straightens up on his one knee. He seems to take a breath before he gets to his feet and turns, looking up the hill. He sees Raven and Freedom and waves. Raven waves back and Freedom barks before the boys hustle by her again, their arms loaded, and start down the hill.

"Help us," Talon tells her, looking back quickly. Raven gets to her feet and saunters over to the tent. She slips inside and gathers the blankets, folds and stacks them neatly, picks them up and slips back out as the boys come back over the crest of the hill for their final loads.

"What about the tent?" Raven asks them as she strides towards the hill crest.

"Mushom said to leave it and he'll come back for it another time," T-Bear tells her. Raven shrugs and carries on until she reaches the hill crest where Freedom still sits. She looks down at Mushom, who reorganizes the sled, and she starts down the hill, careful to keep her footing before she stops and turns back to the dog.

"Come on, Freedom," she says. Freedom whines and she gives him a sympathetic look. "Come on, you can do it," she urges.

Freedom gets up on his front legs and hobbles to the edge of the slope. Gingerly, he lets his paws slide over the edge and, favouring his back right leg heavily, he manages to limp down to Raven.

"Good boy!" she tells him before she turns and continues her descent. Freedom hobbles after as the boys come over the crest with the last of the supplies. They nearly catch up to Raven and Freedom at the bottom. The children drop their loads into the sled and Mushom rearranges them, leaving plenty of room for passengers. "I don't think Freedom can lead your dog team back to the cabin, Mushom," Raven says.

Mushom turns and looks at the injured animal. "I don't think so either," he says before he gently lifts his old dog and places him in the sled. Raven climbs in and cuddles up with Freedom, careful to avoid hurting his leg. "Are you three warm enough?" Mushom asks his grandchildren.

"Yeah," T-Bear responds as Talon nods.

Raven holds up the shoulder of her new coat. "Kohkum and Mom make good clothes," she says.

Mushom smiles and motions to the boys. "T-Bear, Talon, you two take Uncle Peter's sled and follow us."

Talon nods and trots over to Uncle Peter's sled. T-Bear hangs back for a moment. "I won't let you down this time," he tells his mushom in his most grown-up voice.

Mushom nods. "I know you won't."

T-Bear turns and hustles over to Talon at Uncle Peter's sled. "You want to drive?" Talon asks.

T-Bear thinks for a moment. "I've never done it without Mushom behind me," he admits.

Talon shrugs. "You want to or not?"

T-Bear nods and climbs on the back of the sled. Talon gets into the sled and sits down, shifting around until he's comfortable. Seeing the boys in place, Mushom turns to his own dog team, now led by Shadow. "Aiee!" he shouts. Some of the dogs start off and some, like Shadow, hesitate, causing the sled to lurch and stop. Freedom barks at Shadow who turns to look at him. After several more barks from Freedom, Shadow turns to the frozen lake, barks three times, and starts off. With Freedom continuing to bark, the other dogs follow Shadow and the team speeds away.

On the back of Uncle Peter's sled, T-Bear takes a deep breath and he yells too. "Aiee!" Uncle Peter's dogs lunge forward and gain speed quickly, jolting the sled into motion as Talon and T-Bear hang on, T-Bear nearly falling off the back entirely.

"Aiee!" Mushom shouts again.

"Aiee!" T-Bear echoes.

The two dog teams reach top speed and stride easily across this part of the frozen lake, the sleds gliding along behind them. Despite being one dog down, Mushom's dogs maintain the front position, Shadow charging hard, willing the other dogs to keep up. Inside Mushom's sled, Freedom keeps watch as Raven holds him. Talon keeps a steady succession of glances over his shoulder at T-Bear, who holds his own, though his whitish knuckles can't be seen beneath his mitts.

The brief break from the storm is just that − brief. With the two sleds barely five minutes out, as they closely pass an island, the wind picks up and the snow begins to fall. They all notice, but no one wants to point out the obvious. The children watch the storm rebuild its former strength and more. T-Bear glances at the dogs and Mushom in between, but Talon and Raven are mesmerized by the snow as it rides the wind and falls in waves. Only Mushom pays attention to the land, or more precisely the frozen, snow-covered lake. As Raven and Talon pull their blankets closer around their bodies, Mushom catches sight of something in the snow.

"Whoa!" Mushom yells. The dogs slow down, but haltingly and in a disorganized way, until Freedom barks and they come to a complete stop. Mushom rides the boot brake and stops the sled behind them. T-Bear turns his attention away from the clouds and back to the task at hand, his heartbeat increasing rapidly.

"Whoa!" T-Bear screams, jumping on the foot brake with both feet. Uncle Peter's dogs know the command and slow down quickly and in proper unison as Mushom hops off the back of his sled and hustles in the direction they came from, passing Uncle Peter's dogs in the process. When both dogs and sled come to a stop, T-Bear starts breathing again in large gasps. Talon uncovers himself and hops out of the sled.

"What is it?" Talon asks as he chases after Mushom.

Mushom stops and gets down on one knee as Talon runs up behind him. Mushom points at the snow. Despite its new layer, Talon can see them plainly – tracks, and fresh. "Moose?" he asks in a whisper.

Mushom nods and points to the nearby shoreline. "He went in there," he whispers. "So he's close. Probably went to the bay on the other side."

"For protection," Talon muses.

Mushom nods as he scans the island. "Go get my rifle," he finally says and Talon turns and quietly rushes off.

CHAPTER ELEVEN
Two Deep Breaths

Talon hustles over to Mushom's sled as T-Bear steps away from Uncle Peter's. "Why are we stopping?" T-Bear asks. "The storm hasn't died down."

Talon ignores T-Bear as Raven stands up and watches him reach the sled and dig through the supplies. T-Bear walks over.

"What are you looking for?" Raven asks.

Talon pulls out the rifle. "This," he says, "but I can't find the bullets."

"What did you and Mushom see?" T-Bear asks.

"Moose tracks," Talon tells them, "fresh ones."

T-Bear and Raven dig into the sled and start searching. "Where are they supposed to be?" Raven asks.

"I don't know," Talon admits. "We've packed and unpacked so many times I lost track."

Raven stops digging for a moment and looks at Freedom, lying in the sled, breathing hard. "There's something wrong with Freedom," she tells the boys. "And there's something wrong with Mushom too. We need to go back."

"We will, Raven," Talon tells her, "after we find this moose."

The boys keep digging and then Raven spots something tucked under the steering bow. She climbs out of the sled and walks to the back. She digs under the cloth wrapped around the steering bow and pulls out an old leather pouch. Raven opens it up and peeks inside.

"Found them," she calls, staring at two bullets. T-Bear drops the duffel bag he's been searching through and climbs out of the sled. Talon places the rifle's strap over his shoulder.

"Here," Talon says, reaching for the old pouch as he and T-Bear approach the back of the sled. Raven tucks the pouch against her body and turns away from them.

"I'll give them to Mushom," she says.

Talon and T-Bear stop and look at each other. "Fine!" Talon finally says. "Just hurry up."

Raven reaches into her pocket and pulls out the new leather pouch she made. She opens it up and takes the two bullets from the old pouch and puts them in the new. She closes it and turns for the island. "Okay, let's go."

The children see Mushom already walking onto the shore of the island and they hurry after him, leaving the dogs to rest in the snow as the storm rages on. They make good time, but Mushom is already out of sight through the trees as the children scramble up the shore, Talon careful with the rifle, Raven careful with the bullets. They follow Mushom's tracks through the trees, eventually coming out on a rise overlooking a bay. Mushom lies there in the snow, searching the trees on the other side of the bay with a pair of binoculars. The children quietly join him. Talon takes the rifle off his shoulder as Mushom moves the binoculars away from his eyes and pulls the strap over his head. He hands them to Talon, who hands Mushom the rifle.

"Bullets?" Mushom whispers.

Talon motions to Raven. She pulls the new pouch she made out of her coat pocket and holds it out for Mushom. He reaches over and takes the pouch and cradles the rifle in his arms as he takes out the bullets. Raven waits for him to say something about the new pouch, but Mushom goes about his business without seeming to notice.

As Talon uses the binoculars to scan the far trees, Mushom quietly loads the rifle. "Anything?" he asks Talon. Talon shakes his head as he continues to scan. T-Bear watches them, feeling rather left out. Raven crosses her arms. The present she worked so hard on has gone unnoticed.

"Wait," Talon whispers, holding the binoculars still as he studies some movement. The trees are dense, but there are gaps large enough to catch deeper glimpses, and a set of moose antlers enters one. Talon lowers the binoculars and points. "There," he whispers, "near the point."

All eyes focus on the spot Talon indicates, and through the blowing, falling snow and the dense bush, they see the antlers and head of a bull moose on the far side of the bay. Mushom positions himself in the snow and carefully takes aim. Looking through the sight, Mushom carefully lines everything up for the moose's heart, but his vision blurs and he turns away to rub his eyes. He tries again to take aim but his eyes still won't focus properly and he lets out a sigh. T-Bear, Talon and Raven stare at him anxiously.

"What's wrong?" Raven asks.

"My eyes," Mushom says, turning to the boys. "One of you will have to take the shot."

Talon and T-Bear turn and look at each other for a few moments, neither one ready to volunteer. T-Bear finally motions to his cousin. "You've spent more time out on the land," he whispers, "You do it."

"You've shot the rifle just as many times as me," Talon whispers back. "And you're a better shot."

"One of you do it," Mushom whispers to them both, holding the rifle out. T-Bear steps forward and takes the rifle from his mushom. He gets down on his knees, cradling the rifle carefully, then lowers himself onto his stomach and places the rifle butt against his right shoulder, his left arm supporting the barrel.

"One shot, my boy. That's all you need," Mushom tells him.

T-Bear nervously draws two deep breaths and takes aim. Talon and Raven hold their breath as they watch – so does Mushom. T-Bear lines up the sight with the animal as it emerges from the trees and steps out onto the frozen lake, offering a clear shot. Aiming where the animal's heart should be – something Mushom taught them both, T-Bear breathes evenly through his nose as he places his finger over the trigger and gently squeezes until – BOOM!

The powerful rifle fires and recoils, the butt slamming painfully against T-Bear's shoulder and bumping hard against his right cheek, knocking his toque over his eyes. Raven and Talon flinch. The shot echoes across the bay and the moose falls instantly and lies still.

"You got it!" Talon yells as T-Bear pulls his toque off his head.

"I got it?" T-Bear asks before he sees the animal lying motionless on the ice and snow. "I got it!" he repeats enthusiastically.

Talon and Raven cheer as Mushom pats T-Bear on the back and smiles wearily. "We can feed our family now," he says. "We can feed our family now." He slowly lies down on his back and stares at the sky, his breathing shallow as the children watch with alarm.

"Mushom!" Raven yells as Mushom closes his eyes. She leans over him and shakes him by the shoulders.

"Mushom!" she yells again. "Wake up! *Wanska!*" But Mushom remains unconscious. She leans back and looks at the boys, who look just as alarmed as she does. "Now what?" she asks them.

Talon and T-Bear share a look. "Uh..." T-Bear starts to speak, but can't finish.

"Raven," Talon says, "you stay with Mushom. T-Bear and I will bring the dog teams around. We'll set up camp closer to the moose, put up the tent, build another fire, and get Mushom warm."

"What about the moose?" T-Bear asks.

"We'll cover it," Talon says. "There should be another tent and some tarp in Uncle Peter's sled."

"How will we get Mushom down there?" Raven asks.

"Like we got Freedom up that hill," Talon tells her.

T-Bear nods and Talon takes the rifle from his cousin and passes it to his sister. "Just hold it," he tells her as she carefully takes it. "You won't need it, but if you do, you've seen me and T-Bear and Mushom use it lots of times."

Raven nods and the two boys start off. She turns back to her mushom, his eyes still closed, his breathing still shallow. She watches him for a moment, then looks out over the bay at the moose lying on the frozen water. She knows it will be enough to feed everyone for awhile, but Mushom's cabin has never felt so far away.

BACK IN MUSHOM'S CABIN, the teakettle is out and everyone sips at their tin mugs as a pile of crumbs lie on a plate on the table where the bannock used to be. The women stay busy with sewing and darning, but the men sit and brood, feeling useless and helpless, as the wind and the storm rage and howl outside. The silence continues for several more seconds before Jacob can't stand it anymore. He puts his tin mug noisily down on the table and gets to his feet. The others around the table turn and watch as he strides purposefully towards the door.

"Where do you think you're going?" Kohkum Rosalie asks.

"I'm gonna go look again," Jacob answers, pulling his outerwear off the hooks.

"You tried already," Aunt Anne tells him.

"Then I'll try again," he says stubbornly.

As Jacob continues to get ready, Sarah turns and looks at Alphonse. Aunt Anne turns and looks at Uncle Peter. Uncle Peter and Alphonse both let out sighs and put their tin mugs down as well.

"Guess we better go too, then," Uncle Peter says, as though it was his idea. Alphonse nods and they get up and make their way over to the door and join Jacob in getting ready for an excursion into the storm.

"Go west," Kohkum Rosalie tells them without taking her eyes off her sewing.

The men stop and look at her. "They went east," Jacob says.

"I know," Kohkum Rosalie responds. "But Jonas McNabb lives three kilometres west. And he has two dog teams you might be able to borrow."

The women keep their eyes on their work as the men share looks, shrugs, and gestures indicating that Kohkum Rosalie's notion sounds good to them. Ready for the outdoors, they pull up their hoods, open the door, and march into the storm. Alphonse closes the door behind them as they're swallowed by a sea of white. The women keep working as the wind howls in notes that warble, rise, and fall.

"What would they do without us?" Aunt Anne muses.

"Mm-hmm," Sarah sounds in agreement.

THE WIND BLOWS SWIFTLY, making the tall pine trees sway back and forth above the new camp as Talon and T-Bear finish tying the last support to the tree.

"Is Mushom awake yet?"

Raven sticks her head out of the tent. "No," she yells, "but I think he's talking to Kohkum in his sleep." Talon and T-Bear turn and enter the tent to see Mushom covered up and sweating.

"No, we can't trap," Mushom mumbles, his eyes closed, his head moving from side to side. "The animals have to recover first. I will hunt and we will be fine. No, thank you, I'm fine. You go ahead and eat. I have to prepare the dogs." And he stops.

The children look at each other with concern. "He hasn't been eating," T-Bear says.

"He's been letting us eat first," Talon replies.

"Because there is not enough food," Raven adds.

The children think for a moment as they watch their grandfather sleep fitfully. "He needs to eat," T-Bear says. "We have to cook something."

"We'll have to cut up the moose meat," Talon responds as he leans over and reaches for Mushom's belt. Attached to the belt is a hunting sheath and Talon grabs the knife handle and pulls it out, holding the knife up so T-Bear can see. "Mushom's hunting knife," Talon tells him. "Let's go." T-Bear nods and the two boys leave the tent. Raven dunks a cloth into a small pot of melted snow and wrings it out before she dabs Mushom's forehead.

Even though the downed moose isn't far away from the new camp, the going is rough as T-Bear and Talon trudge through the deep snow, leading Uncle Peter's dog team and sled along with them. They reach the large carcass and T-Bear applies the sled's foot brake as Talon kneels, facing the moose's chest, Mushom's knife in hand. T-Bear joins him as the dogs huddle against the wind.

"Did Mushom show you how to do this?" T-Bear asks.

"Once," Talon admits.

He takes a breath as he pictures that day, Mushom inserting the knife, showing him where to cut and why.

Under Talon's careful gaze, Mushom had quartered and gutted the entire moose. Talon knows he won't quarter and gut this one – they just need enough meat to help Mushom regain his strength and for the rest of them to have a good meal. Talon traces a line along the moose's flank, then cuts into the upper portion of its hind leg.

T-Bear watches with a mix of revulsion and resignation. It's messy work and it looks awful, but he knows it's a necessary skill to survive out here. And so he watches and learns, because surviving out here is something Mushom wants them to know. And he realizes it's something they must always know.

Talon cuts the necessary amount of meat with the knack of a quick learner. He drops it on a metal plate and wraps it in a tea towel as T-Bear pulls the tarps and Uncle Peter's canvas tent from the sled and starts to cover up the rest of the moose. Talon puts the meat in the sled and wipes the knife off in the snow before he goes over and helps T-Bear. They weigh the tarps down with logs brought from shore and step back to assess their work.

"Think it'll hold?" T-Bear asks.

Talon shrugs. "Nothing a determined animal couldn't dig through."

"We'll have to guard it," T-Bear says. "We have a rifle."

"With only one bullet," Talon reminds him.

"The animals don't know that," T-Bear says.

Talon nods – true enough. They walk back to Uncle Peter's sled and hop aboard – T-Bear in the sled and Talon at the back, the steering bow in hand.

"Aiee," he says. The dogs stand and assume the proper formation. At the lead, Bear starts off and the team pulls the sled around and back towards the new camp.

BACK AT MUSHOM'S CABIN, the women continue to work, but Sarah and Kohkum Rosalie both turn and look towards the window and the door with worry. "It's getting late," Sarah says. Kohkum Rosalie nods as Aunt Anne puts down her darning and takes one of their hands in each of hers.

"Good thoughts, ladies," Aunt Anne says. "They need our prayers."

Kohkum Rosalie nods but Sarah is harder to convince. Aunt Anne squeezes their hands, when the front door opens and a snow-covered Alphonse steps inside, accompanied by more snow swirling in with the wind. Alphonse shuts the door behind him and lowers his hood. The women see who it is for the first time and Sarah puts her sewing down and walks over to him. Alphonse opens his arms and they hug each other.

"Jonas could only spare one sled?" Kohkum Rosalie asks. Alphonse nods. "And Jacob insisted on going?"

Alphonse nods again. Kohkum Rosalie shrugs. "Maybe it'll make him appreciate the land more," she says. "Maybe he'll let T-Bear come out more often."

Sarah and Alphonse end their hug. "Or maybe he'll never let him come out here again," Sarah says as they move back to the table. They sit and Sarah picks up her sewing as Alphonse picks up his tin mug and holds it out for Kohkum Rosalie. She smiles as she lifts the kettle and pours him more tea.

"Think they're gonna be okay?" Sarah asks her husband. Alphonse nods as he mixes sugar and milk into his cup. He takes a sip as Sarah goes back to her sewing, somehow feeling a little better.

OUT ON THE ISLAND, Talon and T-Bear sit at the fire they built a few metres from the tent, the sled and their bodies shielding it from the storm as much as possible. A pot hangs over the fire from a makeshift tripod of branches and Talon stirs its contents, an empty package of soup mix on the ground beside him. T-Bear turns a chunk of meat he cooks off the end of a stick. The rest of the meat lies tightly wrapped on the plate by the tent door. Talon keeps stirring the soup before he stops and takes a good look at it.

"Think it's ready?" he asks. T-Bear leans over for a look and gives his cousin a nod. Talon takes the pot off the tripod and carefully pours a serving into a metal bowl. He puts the pot of soup beside the teapot, close to the fire to keep it warm, then picks up the metal bowl and carries it over to the tent.

A few metres from the fire, the dogs huddle together and eat their portion of the rich moose meat. Shadow and the others chew ravenously. Freedom chews slowly, but still savours the nourishment. As T-Bear watches, Freedom swallows the piece, gets up, and limps over to the remaining scraps to grab another chunk between his teeth before limping back.

"Soup's ready," Talon says as he steps inside the tent. He puts the bowl on the floor beside Raven, who kneels over her ailing grandfather. "Try and feed him," he tells her.

Raven leans back. "I've never seen Mushom so sick," she says. She picks up a spoon, scoops up a modest amount of soup, and holds it at Mushom's mouth, but Mushom's mouth remains closed. Raven gently pokes at his lips with the edge of the spoon but to no avail. She's still trying when T-Bear steps in with the cooked meat on the stick and watches.

"He needs to be awake if he's going to eat," T-Bear suggests. He digs into Mushom's duffel bag with his free hand and pulls out a small bottle. "Try this," he says. "He showed it to me a few days ago."

"What is it?" Raven asks, looking dubious.

T-Bear pops the lid off with his thumb and they all cringe at the smell and hold their noses. "It's fish guts, bug juice, and some other stuff," T-Bear tells them. "It's for a trap scent. Mushom made a whole bunch last summer. If this won't wake him up, nothing will." He holds it out for Raven. "Put it under his nose."

"Gross!" Raven mutters, her nose wrinkled.

"Could have used some of that stuff earlier," Talon says.

Raven takes the bottle and holds it under Mushom's nose as the boys lean away from the stench. Mushom twitches and stirs, then his eyes flutter open and he slowly lifts his head. "What's going on?" he asks, sniffing the awful odour.

"Mushom!" Raven yells, "You're okay."

"Feeling better, anyway," he answers, realizing what she's holding in her hand.

"We were scared," Raven says, the small bottle of trap scent waving in the air, held between her right thumb and forefinger. Mushom watches it as T-Bear steps in and takes it from her.

"Thought it would wake you up," T-Bear says as he puts the bottle's top back on.

Mushom nods. "It's making my eyes water."

Raven gives Mushom a big hug as Talon nods at Mushom to get his attention. Mushom looks at his grandson over Raven's shoulder.

"You're still weak, Mushom," Talon tells him. "You need to eat. We cooked some moose meat and soup for you."

"Thank you, my boy, but don't worry," Mushom says, trying to put them all at ease. "Mushom was just resting. You go ahead and eat."

The children share looks before T-Bear puts the cooked meat on a plate and puts it down in front of Mushom where he can see it. Raven pushes the bowl of soup to a spot where Mushom can see it too.

"I know in our culture the Elders are served first," T-Bear says with sincere respect. Mushom sees that the children don't intend on backing down and it gives him pause.

"You haven't been eating, Mushom," Talon states. "You need your strength."

"We need your strength," Raven adds. "We need you to get us out of here."

"And there's still a lot of moose meat to pack," T-Bear adds.

For several seconds, Mushom doesn't know what to say. Finally, he smiles at his grandchildren and sits up, pulling the soup and moose meat closer before he closes his eyes and bows his head. The children do the same.

"I thank you, grandfathers, for the wisdom of the children to teach this old man about respect," Mushom begins. "There is still a lot more for me to learn. I am thankful to you for giving me another day to do so. *Aho!*" Mushom opens his eyes and smiles at the children. "Let's eat."

Mushom digs into the food as the children pull out additional utensils and plates, but none make a move until Mushom has taken a good portion for himself. The children slowly dig in and sit back when they've taken their share. As the wind continues to blow, they all eat in silence, Mushom the hungriest of them all. He chews and swallows another satisfying bite and lets out a contented breath as he glances at his grandchildren.

"Did you cover it up?" he asks.

Talon nods. "Used Uncle Peter's tarp and tent, weighed it down with logs."

"Stake them down," Mushom says, "then cover it with snow." Talon and T-Bear nod as they bite into their moose meat. Mushom gauges the time of day by the daylight glow off the canvas walls and ceiling, taking into account the thick cloud cover from the storm. He turns to his granddaughter, who nibbles at her food with enthusiasm.

"Raven," he says. She stops and looks at him and he gives her a warm smile. "Thanks for the beautiful new pouch."

Raven smiles warmly back.

CHAPTER 12
Wapos Bay

As the relentless wind and snow continue their onslaught, Jacob huddles in the sled while Uncle Peter leads Jonas's dog team across this part of the frozen lake. "Aiee!" Uncle Peter wails as they come around a long point on another of the many islands in a large bay. He steers the sled on a course parallel to shore and the entire bay comes into view, partly obscured by the storm.

"Whoa!" Uncle Peter yells. The dogs come to a stop as Uncle Peter manipulates the foot brake.

Jacob sits up and lowers his hood to take a good look around. "Where are we? This place seems familiar."

Uncle Peter takes his hood off as well. "This is Wapos Bay, my boy. This is where your father used to take you hunting when you were just a little guy."

Jacob nods, memories flooding back as he glimpses the land he knew as a boy.

"If the hunting was bad further north, your father would take the long way back through here, and sure enough, he would see something." Uncle Peter shakes his head. "I don't know how he knew, but he did."

"You think they're here?"

"I hope so. Aiee!" The dogs start off again and Jacob pitches backwards as the sled jerks forward. A few seconds later, Uncle Peter has the team gliding at a comfortable speed across the large bay. He and Jacob scan the shoreline. The far side gradually comes into view as they get closer, buffeted by the storm. Finally, the point marking the bay's end reveals itself.

"Whoa!" Uncle Peter yells. The sled comes to a stop. Jacob braces himself and looks back.

"What?" Jacob asks.

Uncle Peter points. "There, on the point."

Jacob looks. "A fire! Is that them?"

"Aiee!" Uncle Peter yells. Covered in snow, the dogs take off again as Jacob holds on and Uncle Peter steers them directly towards the distant blaze.

TALON, T-BEAR, RAVEN, and Mushom lie together under the bearskin blanket, looking sated, as the tent rattles and shakes from the vicious weather.

"Getting your strength back, Mushom?" Raven asks.

Mushom nods. "Mm-hmm!"

Outside, the dogs begin to bark and the children become worried. "Is that something coming after the moose?" T-Bear wonders. Talon climbs out from under the blanket and heads for the door with T-Bear right behind him. Raven and Mushom remain under the blanket.

"Let me know what it is," Mushom calls out to them as they step out.

Through the wind-driven snow, Talon and T-Bear see a dog team approach from the frozen surface of Wapos Bay, as the dogs continue to bark. "It's a dog team!" T-Bear yells towards the tent.

"Who?" Mushom asks from inside.

Talon shakes his head. "They're too far away yet," T-Bear yells as they watch the sled draw near. Soon they can make out the human figures as the dogs continue to drive forward.

"It's Uncle Peter and my dad!" T-Bear shouts. He waves at the approaching sled and his father waves back. Smiling, Talon turns and walks back to the tent as the sled moves off the ice and up to the shore.

Talon sees Mushom and Raven smiling too as he steps inside. Outside, they hear the sled come to a stop nearby. All the dogs bark and greet each other.

"Mushom is sick," they hear T-Bear yelling. "We fed him some moose meat and he seems a bit better now."

"Are you okay?" Jacob asks.

"Yeah," T-Bear says.

As the dogs settle down and the wind continues to rattle and shake the tent, they hear footsteps approach. The tent flap opens and Uncle Peter steps in, covered in snow. Outside, they see Jacob, also covered with snow, hugging T-Bear, who pulls himself away and hustles over to the tent as well. Jacob follows him as Uncle Peter removes his hood and looks at the other two children.

"Are you okay?"

Talon and Raven nod and Uncle Peter kneels down to his brother-in-law. "Your wife is worried sick," he says as he feels Mushom's forehead. "You're too warm. We have to get you back tonight. We'll leave the tent and I'll pick it up tomorrow."

"T-Bear shot his first moose," Mushom tells the two men. Jacob and Uncle Peter turn and stare at the young man with surprise and awe. T-Bear beams, relishing the moment. "The boys cut off some meat and covered the rest, but the tarps have to be staked down and it has to be covered in snow. You can come back tomorrow for that too."

Uncle Peter nods and Jacob ruffles his son's hair with pride, when a thought suddenly hits Raven and she turns to Mushom. "Does this mean we can all stay with you and have Christmas together?"

Mushom smiles. "I believe it does."

"Yay!" Raven yells as the good news sinks in.

"Come on," Uncle Peter tells his brother as he

reaches for him. "Let's get you back and tell the others the good news."

Jacob moves in and they help Mushom struggle to his feet.

Minutes later, the three-dogsled convoy glides across this part of the vast frozen lake, the driving winds and blinding snow in their faces. Uncle Peter leads, with Bear and the rest of his dog team gunning hard and cutting trails anew though the deepening fresh snow, with Raven huddled up inside.

Behind them, Talon drives Mushom's sled with Mushom and Freedom huddled up inside. Shadow is lead dog and he looks confident, charging hard and keeping pace with the team ahead. The rest of Mushom's dogs follow Shadow's lead and keep pace. Even one dog down, they're a match for the others.

Behind Mushom's sled, T-Bear drives Jonas's team while Jacob sits in the sled. With a firm grip on the steering wheel, T-Bear smiles hard as he manoeuvres the team in line with the two ahead. Jacob turns and gives his son a playful scowl and T-Bear laughs. Jacob smiles proudly.

Covered in his bearskin blanket, Mushom watches the trail ahead, obscured as it is by his brother-in-law. Freedom sits with him, staring intently at Shadow and the other dogs on the team. Freedom barks – not a command kind of bark, but a "you're doing good" kind of bark. Gingerly, he lies down over Mushom's lap and places his head on his paws. Mushom pats the old dog, and within moments Freedom is asleep.

BACK AT MUSHOM'S CABIN, Sarah is outside, bundled up against the storm, but not enough to hamper her ability to swing an axe. She swings it high over her head, then down, whipping the axe head with her hands at just the right moment to hit the upright section of log at the maximum amount of speed. The blade strikes dead centre and the log splits in two, both halves falling to the ground amidst several more pieces of wood she has split. Sarah reaches for one of the pieces that just fell and places it back on the larger section of log used as a platform.

As she raises the axe again, Kohkum Rosalie and Aunt Anne, also bundled up against the weather, help Alphonse put a tarp over the front door so it will keep snow from sneaking through the cracks without hampering the door's ability to open. Sarah swings the axe back down and splits the half into quarters, then glances out over the lake, as she has all day. She looks away as she lifts the axe, then stops and looks back at the lake. She squints, searching through the falling snow, and then it becomes clear. Her mouth opens as she points.

"There!" she cries out.

Kohkum Rosalie, Aunt Anne, and Alphonse turn and look. They see the line of three dogsleds snake towards shore. Kohkum Rosalie and Aunt Anne let go of the tarp and scamper over to Sarah, who puts down the axe. The wind catches the tarp and it whips around Alphonse, nearly wrapping him completely.

"The boys are driving," Kohkum Rosalie says, "something must be wrong."

As Alphonse untangles himself from the tarp, the women watch as the dog teams get closer and closer. The kids start waving just before the sleds leave the surface of the lake and climb to shore. The women wave back as they get a closer look. They all seem fine save for one.

"Cyril!" Aunt Anne says. Kohkum Rosalie moves down the trail as Uncle Peter leads his team up the small hill, passing the women and the cabin.

"Whoa!" he calls out as Talon follows next with Mushom's dog team.

"Whoa!" The dogs and the sled come to a stop. Kohkum Rosalie rushes over to Mushom as T-Bear leads Jonas's dog team over the hill.

"Whoa!" T-Bear shouts, the team and the sled stopping behind Talon.

"What happened?" Kohkum Rosalie asks as Sarah and Aunt Anne join her.

"T-Bear shot a moose, that's what happened," Mushom tells her, smiling weakly. The news surprises Alphonse and the women, but Mushom's weakened state has them more concerned.

"He's got a fever," Uncle Peter says.

Kohkum Rosalie puts her bare hand on her husband's forehead and cheeks. "You're flushed," she says before she steps back and motions at Alphonse and Jacob. "Get him inside," she barks at them, in a commanding way. The two men do as they are told and carefully lift Mushom out of the sled as Freedom gets out of the way.

"My dog," Mushom says, worried for Freedom.

"We'll get him too, Dad," Jacob responds, nodding at T-Bear and Talon, who swoop in and carefully lift Freedom from the sled. They all move towards the cabin. Aunt Anne rushes to open the door. Raven watches with Sarah and Uncle Peter as Kohkum Rosalie follows her husband.

"Is Mushom going to be all right, Mom?" Raven asks.

"I hope so, Raven," Sarah says. "I hope so."

The men carry Mushom inside the cabin with Kohkum Rosalie right behind them. Behind her, the boys carry in Freedom.

A BLANKET HANGS, acting as a curtain, and it separates Mushom and Kohkum's sleeping area from the rest of the cabin. Behind the curtain, Mushom is in bed, with Kohkum Rosalie and Aunt Anne huddled over him. Uncle Peter, Alphonse, and Jacob sit quietly at the table, all glancing at the curtain every few moments. Near the wood stove sit Talon, T-Bear, and Raven, their toes warming up near the flames. Sarah kneels beside them, handing out tin mugs of hot tea.

"You know, we were all worried sick," Sarah tells them, her voice low. "Why did you guys leave? What were you thinking?"

Though she speaks in a low voice, the men at the table can still hear and they all turn and look. Talon and Raven glance at their feet as T-Bear looks his aunt in the eyes. "It was my fault, Auntie," he admits. "I thought I was old enough to hunt and trap. I wanted to stay here and learn from Mushom."

Jacob sighs and approaches his son. "I'm sorry, my boy, if I push you too hard at home. If you would like to spend more time out here, then we'll come out here more often. Deal?" He holds his hand out to his son.

T-Bear nods. "Deal!" And he shakes his dad's hand. Jacob smiles and pulls T-Bear towards him for a hug. By the stove, Talon and Raven smile as they watch. So do the other adults.

Kohkum Rosalie and Aunt Anne step out from behind the curtain and everyone turns expectantly. "Mushom is okay," Kohkum Rosalie tells them. "He just pushed himself too hard, without eating, so you children would have enough. He'll be fine, especially now that T-Bear shot his first moose."

Sighs of relief turn into smiles and congratulations for T-Bear as Kohkum Rosalie steps over and kisses him. T-Bear smiles hard, soaking it up, as Kohkum Rosalie kisses Talon and Raven as well. Aunt Anne pulls the blanket down to reveal Mushom in his pajamas, lying in bed and covered in blankets, with his dog Freedom beside him.

"Mushom!" Raven yells, running to the old man's bedside. The other children join her as the adults drift in behind.

Mushom smiles at the lot of them. "Your kohkum says I'll be up and hunting in no time," he announces.

"Of course you will," Raven replies, like she never had any doubt.

Mushom chuckles before he looks down and pets his dog. "It looks like Freedom's days of pulling a sled are over. He'll remain at the cabin from now on."

Freedom licks Mushom's hand as the children and adults alike give the old dog sympathetic looks.

"Ah!" Kohkum Rosalie says, "he'll enjoy my company better anyway." Laughter breaks the silence and the tension. As it slowly dwindles, Kohkum Rosalie grabs her husband's hand. "It's good that the family can spend Christmas together this year."

Mushom nods and turns to T-Bear, Talon, and Raven. "I want to thank you children for the courage and strength you've shown this old man. Merry Christmas!"

"Merry Christmas!" the children say back. They move in and hug their Mushom and he smiles and hugs them back. The adults watch, tears coming to their eyes. Then they all turn to each other.

"Merry Christmas!" they say.

"Merry Christmas!" they say back.

And the little cabin remains warm in the night in the dead of winter on the shore of this part of the vast lake in this part of Northern Saskatchewan...as the storm rages on.

GLOSSARY OF CREE WORDS

Mushom – Grandfather

Wanska – Wake up

Nistow – Brother-in-law

Tenigi – Thank you

Kohkum – Grandmother

Ekosi – That is all

Tansi – Hello

Aho – an exclamation of acknowledgement
with no real English translation

JORDAN WHEELER   DENNIS JACKSON

ABOUT THE AUTHORS

JORDAN WHEELER is the author of, among others, the books *Brothers in Arms, Just a Walk,* and *Chuck in the City.* He has also written and story edited for such shows as *North of 60, The Rez, and Big Bear.* His is currently the Supervising Producer for "renegadepress.com" Jordan, his two children, Cameron and Kaya, and his partner, Rosanna, live in Winnipeg.

DENNIS JACKSON is a film writer-producer, who operates the company Dark Thunder with his wife, Melanie Jackson. He has had extensive experience working with the National Screen Institute. Dark Thunder is developing a "Wapos Bay" television series for the Aboriginal Peoples Television Network. Dennis and Melanie live in Saskatoon with their sons Aaron and Eric.

ACKNOWLEDGEMENTS

I WOULD LIKE TO ACKNOWLEGE all my relations for their patience and understanding in teaching me our Cree culture and way of living. I particularly want to thank my grandfather (mushom), Philip Morin, and my mother, Daisy Renée Jackson, for exposing my imagination to the stories and myths of our culture in northern Saskatchewan.

Dennis Jackson

FROM MANY PEOPLES

Coteau Books began to develop the *From Many Peoples* series of novels for young readers over a year ago, as a celebration of Saskatchewan's Centennial. We looked for stories that would illuminate life in the province from the viewpoints of young people from different cultural groups and we're delighted with the stories we found.

We're especially happy with the unique partnership we have been able to form with the LaVonne Black Memorial Fund in support of *From Many Peoples*. The Fund was looking for projects it could support to honour a woman who had a strong interest in children and their education, and decided that the series was a good choice. With their help, we are able to provide free books to every school in the province, tour the authors across the province, and develop additional materials to support schools in using *From Many Peoples* titles.

This partnership will bring terrific stories to young readers all over Saskatchewan, honour LaVonne Black and her dedication to the children of this province, and help us celebrate Saskatchewan's Centennial. Thank you to everyone involved.

Nik Burton
Managing Editor, Coteau Books

LAVONNE BLACK

My sister LaVonne was born in Oxbow, Saskatchewan, and grew up on a small ranch near Northgate. She spent a lot of time riding horses and always had a dog or a cat in her life. LaVonne's favourite holiday was Christmas. She loved to sing carols and spoil children with gifts. People were of genuine interest to her. She didn't care what you did for a living, or how much money you made. What she did care about was learning as much about you as she could in the time she had with you.

We are proud of our LaVonne, a farm girl who started school in a one-room schoolhouse and later presented a case to the Supreme Court of Canada. Her work took her all over Saskatchewan, and she once said that she didn't know why some people felt they had to go other places, because there is so much beauty here. LaVonne's love and wisdom will always be with me. She taught me that what you give of yourself will be returned to you, and that you should love, play, and live with all your heart.

LaVonne felt very strongly about reading and education, and the LaVonne Black Memorial Fund and her family hope that you enjoy this series of books.

Trevor L. Black, little brother
Chair, LaVonne Black Memorial Fund

LaVonne Black was a tireless advocate for children in her years with the Saskatchewan School Boards Association. Her dedication, passion, and commitment were best summed up in a letter she wrote to boards of education one month before her death, when she announced her decision to retire:

"I thank the Association for providing me with twenty-three years of work and people that I loved. I was blessed to have all that amid an organization with a mission and values in which I believed. School trustees and the administrators who work for them are special people in their commitment, their integrity, and their caring. I was truly blessed and am extremely grateful for the opportunities and experiences I was given."

LaVonne was killed in a car accident on July 19, 2003. She is survived by her daughter, Jasmine, and her fiancé, Richard. We want so much to thank her for all she gave us. Our support for this book series, *From Many Peoples,* is one way to do this. Thank you to everyone who has donated to her Memorial Fund and made this project possible.

Executive, Staff, and member boards of
The Saskatchewan School Boards Association